Wishes and Whispers

ANNIE SEATON

Duckinwilla Days: Book 3

Heartwarming and compelling tales of love, self-discovery, and second chances in the heart of rural Australia.

The Johnson family

Grandmère and Papa: Margot and Robert Johnson

The parents: Hugo and Ellen Johnson

The Johnson siblings:

Charlotte Johnson - Book 1 - *Coming Home*

Julien Johnson -Book 2 - *Secrets and Surprises*

Oliver Johnson - Book 3 – *Wishes and Whispers*

Guy Johnson - Book 4 - *New Beginnings*

Amelia Johnson - Book 5 – *Chasing Dreams*

Lisette Johnson - Book 6 - *Together at Last*

Dedication

For all my country readers.

Chapter 1

The early morning sun lit up the colourful shrubs along the driveway as Oliver heaved the last of the suitcases into the back of the minivan. His muscles strained under the weight of what seemed to be Grandmère's entire wardrobe, packed for their month-long trip to France. He'd already unloaded it from Papa's car when they'd arrived from their house, then Grandmère had insisted on checking each suitcase before she announced they were ready to go into the minivan he and Guy had picked up from Bundaberg early that morning for the travellers to take to Brisbane.

'You'd think they were moving there permanently,' Guy muttered beside him, wiping sweat from his brow. At twenty-seven, Guy was the quieter of the two Johnson brothers, content to let the chaos of family life swirl around him while he focused on the farm's spreadsheets and sugar cane yields. 'They've packed enough clothes to last summer and winter.'

'And Mum's packed enough medication to stock a pharmacy, along with Grandmère's clothes. She's packed enough for a royal tour,' Oliver grunted as he agreed.

'Well, I guess it's not every day they take Grandmère back to France,' Guy said. 'At least the cane harvest is finished. Good timing. We can have a bit of a breather while they're all away.'

'You can. It's just in time for mango season,' Oliver added, glancing toward the orchard. 'I'll be flat out. The early varieties should be ready by the time they come home. I noticed some of the Kensington Prides starting to blush.'

'You and your mangoes,' Guy shook his head. 'Sugar pays the bills, brother.'

'Diversification,' Oliver replied with the automatic response he'd been giving for years. 'Plus, people love those mangoes at the markets.'

The screen door banged open as Ellen, their mother, hurried out to the veranda, clutching her passport and a handful of travel documents; she was wearing the same frazzled expression that had become permanent over the past week of preparations.

'Have either of you seen your father's heart tablets? The little blue ones? He swears he packed them, but you know what he's like since he had the heart attack. Can't find anything.'

'Check the kitchen counter, Mum,' Oliver said with a grin at Guy. 'I saw him sorting pills there last night.'

Charlotte appeared behind their mother; she was holding a packet in her right hand. 'Found them, Mum! They were in the bathroom cabinet, exactly where Dad said they were.' She descended the steps with the confidence of someone who'd been mediating family crises her entire life.

'Why so late, anyway, Charlotte? The trip's later than you planned,' Oliver remarked. 'It's already mid-November. You'll just be back for Christmas.'

'I couldn't take time off from the high school to leave earlier. My Year Twelve class needed me leading up to their final exams. And three weeks in France is hardly excessive,' Charlotte replied. 'We'll be home a week before Christmas. Plenty of time to prepare.'

Their mother smiled, a dreamy look crossing her face. 'And for the wedding preparations, too! I can't believe we'll have two weddings to plan next year.'

'Julien and Emily's renewal of vows hardly counts as a full wedding, Mum,' Charlotte said, although she was smiling too.

'Don't tell Julien that! Emily wants the big celebration they didn't have because they got married at the registry office before they came home from Sydney. And then your wedding in May, Charlotte.' Ellen sighed happily. 'So much to look forward to.'

Greg, Charlotte's fiancé of almost a year, came in from the kitchen with an armload of snacks. 'Road trip essentials,' he explained with a wink as he passed Oliver. 'Your mum's worried they'll starve on the three-hour drive to Brisbane.'

'More likely they'll miss the plane because they can't close the door on the minivan,' Oliver said under his breath, causing Greg to chuckle.

The house hummed with the excitement of six people preparing to depart for a long-awaited trip. Grandmère fussed over her travel outfit—a smart navy pantsuit that made her look a decade younger than her seventy years—while Papa pretended to listen to her concerns about plane food. At eighty-two, he'd maintained the ability to tune out selectively, a skill Oliver deeply respected and aspired to master himself one day. With three sisters, he'd been fighting a losing battle since he was in kindergarten.

'*Ooh la la*, to think I will see my cousins tonight after all these years!' Grandmère exclaimed, her hands fluttering excitedly. 'My little village near Lyon, it will have changed so much. When I left as a girl of nineteen to marry your grandfather, I never imagined it would be so long before I returned.'

Papa smiled indulgently. 'Margot, you've told this story every day for the past month.'

'And I will tell it every day until we land in Paris!' she declared, her accent growing stronger with her excitement. 'The family château—well, not really a château, more a large stone house— but the vineyards, the lavender fields. Oliver, you should be coming with us! The French countryside would put hairs on your chest.'

'I think I have enough hair already, Grandmère,' Oliver replied with a grin.

'Oliver!' His father called from the study. 'While you're waiting around, can you please check this itinerary for me again? I'm not sure if we're supposed to transfer in Singapore or Dubai.'

Oliver rolled his eyes as he walked across the living room of the farmhouse to the study, which he and Guy shared with Dad. While they were at school, they had done their homework at the scrubbed timber kitchen table, but when they started working on the farm, Dad had bought them a desk each. It was cramped, but a lot of good planning had taken place in that room over the past few years. He took the crumpled printout from his father's hand. 'Dubai, Dad. It's highlighted right here.' He pointed to the fluorescent yellow streak across the page. 'And Greg has his copy, so it's all under control.' Oliver knew that Dad was nervous about the trip; he'd never been overseas before, but his reluctance to go had been overruled by Grandmère.

'I want my only child to see his heritage, please, Hugo.'

Between Mum—and her desire to see Europe—and Grandmère, Dad had been off to the local post office getting his passport photo taken before he could think twice.

He nodded, running a hand through his thinning grey hair. 'Right, right. Just checking. And you boys have the farm schedule? The irrigation repairs are due next Thursday.'

'We've been over this three times, Dad. Don't stress,' Oliver said patiently. 'Guy's made a spreadsheet. The farm will survive without your supervision for four weeks.'

'Four weeks,' his father repeated, the reality seemingly hitting him for the first time. 'That's a long time to be away from the cane.'

Oliver squeezed his father's shoulder. 'It's only been three years since you handed the running of the General Store to Julien. The cane survived then; it won't even notice you're gone.'

A high-pitched squeal from the kitchen interrupted them, followed by Grandmère's rapid-fire French. Oliver hurried out to find her clutching Papa's arm, both beaming at a tablet held by Amelia.

'Lisette' FaceTimed from Melbourne,' Amelia explained, her hair—currently dyed in vibrant stripes of teal, purple, and pink— catching the morning light as she put the tablet on the dining room table and tilted the screen toward Oliver. 'She wants to wish you all a safe trip.'

Lisette's face filled the screen, her formerly harsh features softened both by the video quality and the gradual mellowing she'd undergone in the past year. Once she and Charlotte had sorted their differences, she'd been much happier. 'You're all looking very smart for economy class travellers,' she teased, her artwork visible in the background. 'Oli, you actually combed your hair for their departure. I'm impressed.'

Oliver ran a self-conscious hand through his dark curls. 'Someone had to look presentable for the neighbours. They'll think we're selling the farm if the whole family leaves at once.'

'Are you sure you can't come join us in France, Lisette?' their mother asked, leaning in front of the tablet screen. 'The invitation from your father's cousins included everyone. And you'd be back in time for Christmas. We could make sure of that.'

Lisette's smile was genuinely regretful. 'The gallery exhibition opens in three weeks, Mum. I can't leave now.' In the year since moving to

Melbourne, Lisette had transformed from the sharp-tongued sister to a surprisingly successful art gallery assistant. 'Besides, someone has to check in on the farm boys and make sure they're not living on beer and beef pies.'

'I'll be doing that. I'm taking over the cooking,' Amelia said smugly.

'Heaven help the boys,' Lisette quipped.

'We'll FaceTime you from Paris,' Charlotte promised, squeezing into view. 'You can virtually tour the Louvre with us.'

'Better than nothing,' Lisette agreed before her gaze sharpened on Oliver. 'Though speaking of virtual, Oli, I've been meaning to talk to you about online dating. Amelia mentioned you're still stubbornly single.'

Oliver shot Amelia a filthy look, which she answered with an innocent smile and a flutter of her purple-mascaraed eyelashes. 'Lisette, it's not the time,' he muttered.

'When is the time, then?' Amelia piped up, handing the tablet to Charlotte and crossing her arms. 'You're almost twenty-five, Oli. Your idea of socialising is nodding at the fertiliser delivery guy when he drives out in his truck.'

'I socialise heaps,' he protested weakly.

Guy looked up from his phone for the first time that morning. 'What's happening?'

'Amelia and Lisette are tag-teaming Oli about his love life,' Charlotte explained.

Guy immediately returned to his screen. 'Cane prices are dropping again. Not good.'

'Coward,' Oliver glared at him. 'Where's some brotherly solidarity?'

'He needs to get with it,' Amelia declared, turning to address the family audience. 'It's the twenty-first century! People don't meet in supermarket aisles anymore. They swipe.'

'I don't want to swipe anyone,' Oliver said firmly. 'And maybe if you spent less time on dating apps and more time on keeping a natural hair colour, you wouldn't have gone through three boyfriends since the Crush Festival.'

Amelia patted her multicoloured hair proudly. 'My parrot hair, as you so lovingly call it, is a conversation starter. And for your information, I've been seeing Myron for three weeks now.'

'Ooh, a record,' Lisette chimed in. 'Play the field, sister. Good to see.' She frowned. 'Strange name, though.'

'Who's Myron?' Ellen asked, momentarily distracted from her travel checklist. 'You haven't mentioned him before.'

'The new barista at the store,' Amelia said. 'Tall, makes amazing latte art.'

Grandmère perked up. 'The one with the tattoos of the little birds? Very handsome. French men appreciate artistic flair, you know. My cousin Antoine had a magnificent moustache that he waxed into points.'

'He draws kingfishers in the foamed milk,' Charlotte confirmed. 'Already a customer favourite. Julien's really happy with him.'

'And Amelia,' Oliver teased.

'We are going to stop by the store on the way out, aren't we?' Ellen frowned. 'To say goodbye to Julien and Emily.'

When no one answered her, she walked away from the table where Amelia had the tablet propped up against the jug of flowers.

'Well, Oli could use some colour himself,' Lisette's voice chimed in from the forgotten video connection. 'Maybe some highlights? You've got that whole brooding farmer look going, but a few golden streaks might soften it.'

Oliver's mouth fell open in horror. 'I am not dyeing my hair.'

'It would bring out your eyes,' Amelia agreed seriously, studying his face. 'And distract from that permanent furrow between your eyebrows.'

'There is no furrow,' Oliver protested, consciously relaxing his forehead.

'There absolutely is,' Lisette countered. 'It's been there since you were twelve and Dad put you in charge of the irrigation schedules.'

'Responsibility etches itself on the face,' Papa contributed sagely from an armchair, clearly enjoying the family entertainment.

'Well,' Lisette sighed dramatically from the tablet, 'at least Mum'll have two weddings next year. Though it won't be yours, Oli, at this rate.'

'Lisette!' their mother scolded, though she looked more amused than upset.

'What? I'm just saying we shouldn't hold our breath. Unless—' Lisette's voice took on a sly tone. 'Has that market girl shown up again? The one with the amazing laugh that Oli wouldn't shut up about last year?'

Oliver's face burned. 'Her name is Sarah, and no, she hasn't.'

'Shame,' Lisette said, not sounding particularly sympathetic. 'Though perhaps we should be thankful. I heard she has a child, and we all know how Oli feels about noise.'

'We're getting off track,' Amelia said, whipping out her phone. 'I've been compiling a list of eligible women in the district for him. There's Melissa Harper, the new preschool teacher at Duckinwilla Primary. She's got that whole wholesome, "I love children".'

'Perfect for a man who scowls at primary school lamington sellers,' Lisette added.

'I bought a dozen at the last markets,' Oliver defended himself.

'Under duress,' Charlotte reminded him. 'After the little girl cried.'

'She was very persuasive,' Oliver muttered.

'In my village when I was a girl and being courted,' Grandmère interjected excitedly, 'the matchmaker would have paired you with the baker's daughter by now. A good strong woman who can help with the mango harvest!' She clasped her hands together. 'Perhaps I will find you a nice French girl while we are there!'

Amelia continued undeterred. 'Then there's Kaitlyn Webb, who runs that new crystal stall at the weekend markets. Very spiritual, but she makes her own bread and mentioned wanting a vegetable garden.'

The mention of the markets made Oliver's stomach tighten unexpectedly. It had been almost a year since he'd met Sarah at the Dunmora markets during last season's mango harvest. They'd talked for nearly an hour while she admired his fruit and he admired . . . well, everything about her. He'd taken her number, written on a docket that had somehow vanished before he'd made it home. He'd returned to the Dunmora markets the following weekend, but her craft site had been empty. He'd continued visiting those markets for weeks, but she never returned, and he'd eventually given up looking for her there.

'Earth to Oliver,' Amelia was saying, snapping her fingers in front of his face. 'You disappeared there for a second.'

'Forget all that dating stuff; it's time you should get on the road,' he covered quickly, addressing the travellers. 'It's a long drive to Brisbane, and the peak hour traffic could be pretty bad.'

His father glanced at his watch and let out a startled exclamation. 'Oli's right! We need to leave in the next ten minutes or we'll hit peak hour.'

The next few minutes dissolved into a flurry of last-minute checks, bathroom visits, and tearful hugs. Oliver found himself pulled into embrace after embrace, doling out promises to water houseplants and collect mail at Grandmère and Papa's place, and then assuring Dad that he and Guy would keep the farm running smoothly.

'And think about what we said,' Amelia whispered sideways to Oliver after she'd hugged everyone goodbye. 'Life's too short to spend it talking only to sugar cane.'

'We'll have that dating profile set up before they reach France,' Lisette promised from the tablet, which Charlotte was now carrying to the minivan.

'Don't you dare,' Oliver called after them, but his protest was lost in the commotion of final goodbyes.

Guy appeared at his shoulder as they watched the minivan finally pull away, arms waving from every window. 'Thank God. Peace and quiet for a month,' he said with quiet satisfaction.

Oliver nodded, already mentally listing the tasks awaiting them in the fields. 'Peace, quiet, and about two thousand acres of cane, and six hundred mango trees that need our attention.'

'I'll keep you pair in line,' Amelia said. 'What do you want for dinner tonight?'

'Steak?' Guy asked with a hopeful smile. 'And don't forget to leave time for the highlights in Oli's hair.'

Oliver elbowed him hard in the ribs, but couldn't help grinning as they turned back towards the house. The place felt suddenly enormous and empty with just the three of them. But peacefully quiet.

'I'll go and take some steaks out of the freezer in the shed.' Amelia disappeared through the breezeway.

For all Oliver's protests, a small part of him wondered if Amelia might be right. Maybe it was time to 'get with it,' whatever that meant. He was almost twenty-five. But not with highlights. God forbid. He shuddered. And definitely not with swiping on some dating app.

Oliver's thoughts drifted back to the markets, to Sarah's laugh and the way she'd tucked her hair behind her ear while examining a particularly perfect mango. He'd noticed she didn't wear a wedding ring, and when he'd carefully asked about Jett's father, a shadow had passed across her face before she simply said, 'It's just the two of us.' He hadn't pressed further—some stories weren't meant for first meetings between strangers at market stalls.

As he headed to the kitchen to put the kettle on before he and Guy went back out to the fields, he remembered how he'd looked for Sarah every weekend for a month before giving up, assuming she'd moved on or away.

Maybe his sisters were right about one thing—it was time for him to move on, too.

A little voice nagged away at him in a whisper. *But I don't want to.*

But for the time being, he and Guy had a farm to run as well as keeping an eye on Amelia while the oldies were away.

Chapter 2

The first week without the family passed in a blur of work. Oliver threw himself into the cane fields with a focus that even Guy commented on—once, briefly, late on Tuesday night before returning to his spreadsheets. With Dad gone, they'd both taken on extra responsibilities: Guy managing the books and coordinating with the sugar mill, Oliver overseeing the day-to-day operations and the small crew of seasonal workers they'd hired to help with the pre-harvest preparations. He hadn't had time to look at his mangoes all week. The mango harvest was only a couple of weeks away, and he was hoping that there would be no storms before he could get them picked.

Guy was on the back porch that evening, guitar in hand, softly picking out a melody as the sunset painted the cane fields in gold. It was a side of his brother few people saw—the quiet musician who found solace in music after long days of practical farm work.

'Sounds good,' Oliver commented, dropping onto the old sofa chair beside him. 'New song?'

Guy's fingers stilled on the strings. 'Just something I've been working on.' He had a private intensity that contrasted with Oliver's more straightforward approach to life. Where Oliver was practical and present, Guy seemed to live half in his head, observing the world with a thoughtfulness that was often mistaken for detachment.

'The seasonal crew seems solid this year,' Oliver remarked, changing the subject. 'That new worker—Elena?—she really knows her way around irrigation systems.'

Something flickered across Guy's face. 'Elena Santiago. She's worked three harvests on the big Mackay plantations. Overqualified for what we're paying, to be honest.'

'Then why's she here?'

Guy shrugged, but there was a tension in his shoulders that hadn't been there before. 'Said she wanted to learn about smaller-scale sustainable farming. She's got some interesting ideas about water conservation.'

'Since when do you discuss farming philosophy with the seasonal help?' Oliver asked, surprised.

'Since Dad put me in charge of the books,' Guy replied, putting his guitar against the wall. 'Someone has to think about the farm's future beyond the next harvest.'

Before Oliver could ask what he meant, Guy stood up. 'I should finish those spreadsheets. The mill wants our projections by Friday.'

By Friday evening, Oliver's muscles had reached that state of fatigue where his body seemed to creak with exhaustion. He'd spent the day replacing irrigation lines along the eastern boundary, the sun burning his shirtless back as he dragged sections of pipe through the thick mud. When he finally trudged back to the farmhouse at sunset, his clothes were filthy, his boots caked with rich, dark soil, and his muscles aching.

'Pub tonight? It's Friday,' Guy asked, already dressed in clean jeans and a button-down shirt, his hair still damp from the shower.

Oliver mustered enough energy to shake his head. 'I'm knackered, mate. You go out, though.'

'Suit yourself,' Guy had replied with a shrug. 'There's a new band playing. Might be decent.'

'Tell me all about it tomorrow.' Oliver managed a weary smile. 'I'm going to spend tomorrow in the mangoes.'

Guy grimaced but nodded. 'Fair enough. Don't wait up.'

Now, freshly showered and horizontal on his bed, Oliver stared at the ceiling fan spinning lazily above him. The house was quiet—Guy at the pub, Amelia presumably out with Myron the barista. He'd been too tired to eat a proper dinner, settling instead for a toasted sandwich eaten standing at the kitchen counter. His eyelids had just begun to droop when his bedroom door burst open.

'You're not asleep yet, are you?' Amelia demanded, flicking on the light. 'It's only eight o'clock on a Friday night, for goodness' sake! How old are you, Oli? Anyone would think you were on the downside of fifty. Come on, wake up.'

'Why?' Oliver groaned, throwing an arm over his eyes. 'All right, all right. I'm getting there.'

'Well, hurry up and get there. I have

something to show you.' Amelia bounced onto the foot of his bed with an enthusiasm that rocked the mattress.

'Whatever it is, it can wait until morning,' he mumbled. 'I thought you were out anyway.'

'I thought you'd gone to the pub with Guy, but I guess that was a silly thing to hope for. I was in my room doing this.'

'Amelia, I'm stuffed. Go away. I'll look at whatever it is in the morning.'

'No, it absolutely cannot wait until then.' She was practically vibrating with excitement, her laptop balanced on her knees at the foot of his bed. 'Ta-da! Sit up and look at this.'

Oliver squinted at the screen she'd thrust toward him. It took several seconds for his tired brain to process what he was seeing. When it did, he bolted upright, fatigue forgotten.

'What. Have. You. Done?' His eyes widened in disbelief.

Filling the screen was a dating profile. His dating profile, if the name 'Oliver Johnson' and a startlingly flattering photo of him at the Crush Festival in October were anything to go by. He was smiling in the picture—so rare an occurrence that he couldn't even remember who'd taken it—and the sunset lighting made him look almost handsome.

'CountryConnect.com.au,' Amelia announced proudly. 'The premier dating site for rural singles!'

'Delete it,' he said immediately. 'Right now.'

'I will not,' she said, pulling the laptop back protectively. 'You need this, Oli. I'm tired of watching you mope around the farm like some tragic hero in a period drama.'

'I don't mope! And I've never watched a period drama in my life.'

'You absolutely do mope. You've been moping for a year since that market girl ghosted you.'

Oliver felt a flare of irritation. 'Sarah didn't ghost me. I lost *her* number.'

'So you say.' Amelia rolled her eyes. 'And yet somehow you've managed not to meet anyone else in an entire year.'

'I've been busy,' he protested. 'The mangoes and the cane—'

'The mangoes, the cane, the mangoes,' she

mimicked. 'Dad has the same excuse, and he and Mum have been married for thirty years! You need a life outside of dirt, sugar cane and mangoes, Oli.'

He reached for the laptop, but she twisted away. 'Show me what ridiculous things you've written about me.'

Amelia relented, angling the screen so he could read it. Oliver's eyes widened as he scanned the profile:

Who am I? I'm Oliver Johnson, twenty-five, Duckinwilla Creek, Queensland.

About Me: Third-generation cane farmer with a secret talent for baking the perfect scone and naming every constellation in the night sky. When I'm not working the land my family has owned for generations, you'll probably find me lost in a good book or taking long walks along the creek with my dog, Ruby. I value honesty, hard work, and people who can appreciate the simple beauty of a Queensland sunset.

Looking For: Someone genuine who understands that the land demands commitment but knows that true partnerships make the work worthwhile. Must love open spaces, starry nights, and the occasional mud on the kitchen floor (I always clean it up eventually). Bonus points if you can spot the Southern Cross faster than I can.

'I don't bake scones,' was all Oliver could manage. He felt as though his eyes were about to pop out of his head. He drew in a big breath. 'And Ruby? What self-respecting cane farmer would have a working dog called Ruby? Honestly, Amelia, that's absolute tripe. Take it down.'

She shook her head. 'Grandmère said you helped her bake scones once when you were twelve. Close enough.'

'And I don't take walks along the creek! When would I have time for that? And I don't have a Ruby. What sort of dog would that be?'

She giggled. 'Oh, I thought a little fluffy wide 'oodle' of some sort might sound enticing.'

Oliver was speechless.

'Details don't matter,' Amelia waved a hand. 'The point is to sell the fantasy, Oli. Truth is overrated. No one wants to date a man whose profile says 'Works seven days a week, collapses into bed by nine, couldn't tell the difference between a good conversation and a fence post.'

'I talk to people!'

'Grunting at the feed store doesn't count.' She scrolled down. 'Look at the rest!'

Oliver scanned the rest of the profile with growing horror. Under "Interests", Amelia had listed hiking, astronomy, classic literature, and— most bewilderingly— "artisanal baking."

'When's the last time you read anything that wasn't a farming manual?' she challenged before he could speak.

'I'm reading that thriller Greg lent me,' he said defensively.

'The one that's been on your bedside table since your birthday?'

He glanced guiltily at the dusty paperback. 'I'm a slow reader.'

'You're a non-reader,' she corrected. 'But women like men who read, so now you read.'

Oliver fell back against his pillows with a groan. 'This is ridiculous. No one's going to believe any of this.'

'Oh, they already do,' Amelia said cheerfully, clicking to another screen. 'You've got three matches!'

'What?' Oliver shot upright again. 'Bloody hell, sis. What have you done?'

'Three women have already expressed interest,' she announced triumphantly. 'And I've replied to all of them.'

'You've been pretending to be me?' His voice rose to a pitch it hadn't hit since puberty.

'Just to get the ball rolling,' she assured him. 'Jessica wants to meet for coffee next week. She seems nice—kindergarten teacher, likes hiking, has a cute Labrador.'

'Oh. My. God.' Oliver buried his face in his hands. 'This is a nightmare. You are a nightmare.'

'No, this is your chance to actually meet someone,' Amelia insisted. 'Look, Oli.' Her voice softened. 'I know you work hard. I know the farm is important to you. But you can't spend your whole life waiting for some girl from the markets to magically reappear. She's moved away, or she's got a new job, or she's found a man.'

Oliver's shoulders slumped. 'It's not just about Sarah.'

'Then what is it about?'

He sighed, trying to express something he rarely thought about. 'Dating is . . . complicated. Working on the farm with Dad and Guy takes all my time, and most women don't understand that. I've got enough on my plate without adding relationship drama.'

Amelia tapped the screen. 'That's why online dating is perfect. You can be upfront about your lifestyle. These women know you're a farmer—they're specifically looking for someone like you.'

Oliver squinted at her suspiciously. 'Why do you care so much about my love life?'

'Because you're my big brother and I love you,' she said simply. 'And because you're miserable, even if you won't admit it.'

'I'm not—'

'You are,' she interrupted. 'I see how you look when Charlotte and Greg visit, or when Julien and Emily come over. You want what they have, but you're too scared to do anything about it.'

Oliver fell silent, unable to find a convincing denial.

'Just one coffee,' Amelia wheedled. 'With

Jessica. Next Friday afternoon at The Bean Counter at Dunmora. I've already set it up. I didn't think you want to go to the General Store. Too much family, and locals to interrupt the "getting to know you bit".'

'You're unbelievable,' he muttered.

'I'm efficient,' she corrected with a grin. 'And if it doesn't work out, there's always Brittany—she's a bookkeeper who likes gardening—or Danielle, who—'

Oliver ran a hand through his damp hair and interrupted. 'Did you ask anyone else about me?'

Amelia's hesitation was brief but noticeable. 'Well—'

'Amelia,' he groaned. 'Who else?'

'I might have mentioned to Kaitlyn at the primary school that my brother was single.'

Oliver stared at her in disbelief. 'Kaitlyn Miller? The one who coaches the under-fives football?'

'That's the one,' Amelia nodded. 'She's pretty, she's sporty, and she's good with kids.'

'And?'

'And what?'

'What did she say?' Oliver demanded,

suddenly feeling strangely curious.

Amelia examined her fingernails. 'I won't tell you what she said, though.'

Something in her tone made Oliver sit up straight. 'What did she say?'

'It doesn't matter.'

'Clearly it does, or you wouldn't have brought it up,' he countered. 'What did she say?'

Amelia sighed dramatically. 'She said, and I quote, "If a man has to get his sister to ask her friends to go out with her brother, there's something wrong with the brother".'

Indignation heated his face. 'There's nothing wrong with me!'

'That's what I told her!' Amelia said, patting his knee. 'I said you were just shy and busy and terrible at talking to women.'

'Not helping,' he muttered.

'But that's exactly my point, Oli,' she continued, her expression growing serious. 'You're a great guy, but you never put yourself out there. You hide behind the farm and your responsibilities. You need to show people—women—who you really are.'

Oliver sighed, recognising the futility of

further argument. 'One coffee. That's it. And then you delete this profile.'

'If you absolutely hate it, I'll *consider* deleting it,' Amelia hedged.

'Amelia.' He took a deep breath in an attempt to calm down.

'Fine! If you go on the date and truly hate it, I'll delete the profile,' she conceded. 'But you have to actually try, Oli. No scowling, no checking your watch every five minutes, and absolutely no talking about irrigation systems unless she asks.'

'I don't only talk about irrigation,' he protested weakly.

'Last Christmas dinner, you spent forty-five minutes explaining drip systems to Uncle Bob.'

'He asked!'

'He was being polite! His eyes were glazed over when he went for another beer.' Amelia closed the laptop with a decisive snap. 'Tuesday, four o'clock. Wear that blue shirt Charlotte got you for your birthday—it makes your eyes look less murderous.'

'My eyes don't look murderous,' Oliver grumbled.

'They absolutely do when you're talking to women you don't know,' she said, standing up. 'It's like you're trying to scare them off before they can reject you.'

'That's ridiculous.'

'Is it, though?' Amelia paused at the door. 'Just . . . try, okay? For me. And maybe a little bit for you.'

After she left, Oliver lay back on his bed, staring at the ceiling fan. A date. With a kindergarten teacher. Who thought he was an artisanal baker with a passion for astronomy.

This was going to be a disaster.

He rolled onto his side, catching sight of the moon through his window. Despite himself, he found his thoughts drifting to Sarah again. What would she be doing right now? Had she left the district? Found someone else? He'd looked for her at the markets for weeks after losing her number, but her craft stall site had remained stubbornly empty. He hadn't had the confidence to seek her out.

Coward, that persistent little voice whispered.

Maybe Amelia was right. Maybe it was time

to move on. With a deep sigh, Oliver closed his eyes, too exhausted to worry about it anymore. His last thought before sleep claimed him was that he really, really hoped Jessica wouldn't ask him about constellations.

Chapter 3

Oliver wiped his brow with the back of his hand, leaving a smear of dirt across his forehead. The morning had been productive—two irrigation lines fixed, a fence mended where a fallen branch had taken out a section during last week's storm, and a start on clearing the access road to the eastern paddocks. Now, with the midday sun beating down mercilessly, he'd retreated to the shade of the equipment shed for lunch. Guy had gone to Bundaberg for the day to a grower's meeting.

He unscrewed his thermos and took a long drink of lukewarm water before unwrapping the ham and cheese sandwich Amelia had packed. His phone buzzed in his pocket, and he pulled it out with dirt-stained fingers to find a notification from CountryConnections.

'Jessica has sent you a message!'

Oliver groaned. He'd almost managed to forget about Monday's upcoming coffee date, but there it was, a bright, cheerful reminder that at four o'clock on Monday afternoon, he'd be sitting across from a kindergarten teacher who expected him to be an astronomy-loving baker with a penchant for long walks, and with a fluffy dog, to add insult to injury.

Against his better judgement, he opened the app, wincing at the profile photo Amelia had chosen. It really was a good picture of him—caught mid-laugh at last year's Crush Festival, wearing a clean blue shirt (Charlotte's doing) and looking far more approachable than he felt most days.

Jessica's message was short and friendly: 'Looking forward to meeting you at The Bean Counter on Monday! I'll be wearing a yellow dress. See you at 4!'

Oliver grimaced. She sounded nice. Which made what he was about to do even worse. He typed out a reply, his thumbs hovering over the keys.

'Something's come up on the farm. Need to reschedule.'

His finger hovered over 'Send' for a long moment before he deleted the message with a sigh. Amelia would know he was lying. She'd probably already texted Jessica from his phone anyway, judging by the earlier messages he'd scrolled through with mounting horror. His supposed enthusiasm for Jessica's classroom garden project had been expressed with far more exclamation marks than he'd used in his entire life.

He shoved the phone back in his pocket and took a bite of his sandwich, chewing mechanically as he stared out across the cane fields.

When he'd finished eating, Oliver reluctantly checked his watch. One forty-five. He had the whole weekend to prepare mentally. Amelia had insisted on a Monday date, claiming it would "start his week off right," though Oliver suspected it was just because Jessica wasn't available on the weekend.

'This is ridiculous,' he muttered to himself as he packed away his lunch things.

One coffee. He could survive one coffee, he told himself.

Back at the house, he found Amelia waiting for him, a knowing smile on her face.

'What are you doing home?'

'I only work mornings on Fridays. Haven't you ever noticed?' She held up one hand. 'Don't bother answering. Unless it grows in a cane field or on a tree, you don't notice.'

'That's a bit harsh.'

His sister shrugged and pulled a face. 'Maybe harsh, but true.'

Oliver frowned. Surely, she was exaggerating.

'I've laid out your blue shirt for Monday,' Amelia continued, pointing toward his bedroom. 'And there are clean jeans on the bed. You can't wear what you usually wear.'

'I was going to wear what I've got on,' he said, gesturing to his dirt-streaked work clothes.

Amelia's eyes widened in horror. 'You will not sabotage this date before it even starts, Oliver Johnson. Shower. Blue shirt. Clean jeans. Don't even think about it.'

'I was joking. Where's your sense of humour?'

'You were not.'

'I was. And it's not a date, it's a coffee.'

'It's a date,' she insisted, crossing her arms. 'And you're going to be charming and talk about something other than mango varieties.'

That made him think of Sarah. She'd been

fascinated when he'd told her about the different varieties last year at the Dunmora markets. Shame she'd never turned up again after that first time.

'Fine,' Oliver agreed reluctantly. 'I'll be charming and agreeable and wear the blue shirt. But just this once.'

'That's all I ask,' Amelia said with a triumphant smile.

Oliver rolled his eyes but didn't argue.

Forty minutes later, freshly showered and wearing the blue shirt that Charlotte swore brought out his eyes, Oliver trudged out to his ute. He stopped short when he saw it, noticing for the first time in weeks just how filthy it was. A layer of dust coated every surface, and the tray was littered with irrigation parts, rope, and what appeared to be a work boot missing its partner.

Maybe this would work in his favour. One look at his vehicle, and Jessica would realise he wasn't the polished, poetry-reading type his profile suggested. She might even make her excuses and leave early. He could offer to drive her home, and the state of his ute would ensure she never wanted to see him again.

The thought brightened his mood considerably as he climbed behind the wheel and headed toward Bargara Beach.

***

On the other side of Bundaberg in the beachside suburb of Bargara, Sarah Matthews carefully arranged her handcrafted jewellery on a display board and then placed her soaps to one side. The Friday afternoon-evening markets had just opened, and early visitors were beginning to wander between the stalls set up along the foreshore park.

'Mummy, can I put these out?' Four-year-old Jett held up a tray of beaded bracelets, his small face serious with the responsibility.

'Of course, sweetie. Right over here.' Sarah cleared a space on the folding table, watching as her son meticulously arranged the bracelets by colour—a system he'd devised himself and insisted upon at every market.

'Is the mango man coming today?' Jett asked, his eyes scanning the growing crowd.

Sarah's heart gave its now-familiar twinge. 'No, sweetheart. I don't think so.' How long would it take to forget about the man she'd been so attracted to last year? Jett hadn't forgotten him.

Maybe forever, her heart whispered.

'But he might,' Jett insisted with the unwavering optimism of childhood. 'He said I could try the yellow ones next time.'

'The *Nam Doc Mai* variety,' Sarah said automatically, the name forever etched in her memory from Oliver's enthusiastic description. 'And yes, he might come, but the mango season's only just starting. The mangoes probably aren't ready yet.'

Jett nodded sagely, accepting this explanation as he had a dozen times before. 'When they're ready, he'll come.'

Sarah busied herself with adjusting her earring display, using the moment to compose her features. It had been nearly a year—almost to the day—since she'd met Oliver Johnson when he'd set up his mango stall at the market beside her craft stall at Dunmora. One perfect afternoon of conversation had left her smiling for days afterwards, until the realisation set in that he wasn't going to call. He probably didn't want to date someone with a child.

She'd given him her number. He'd written it down carefully on a docket, tucking it into his wallet with a promise to call that weekend. When Sunday night came with no word, she'd made excuses for him—he was busy with the farm, he'd lost the paper, his phone had died. By the following weekend, she'd decided not to go to the country markets; he obviously hadn't intended to call her.

'Stop it,' she whispered under her breath. 'It was one conversation.'

But what a conversation it had been. Oliver had been different from the men she usually met—quieter, more thoughtful, with a passion for his mangoes that had been unexpectedly endearing. He'd spent twenty minutes showing Jett how to tell when different varieties were perfectly ripe, then given him a specially selected fruit "just for being such a good listener." Jett had been enchanted, and if she were honest, so had she.

Perhaps it was because Jett was at an age where he was becoming more aware of other family structures. Lately, he'd been asking more questions about his father—questions that grew increasingly difficult to answer in ways a four-year-old could understand.

'Did my daddy like mangoes too?' he'd asked last week after they'd bought some from the grocery store.

'I think he would have,' Sarah had answered honestly. 'Your daddy liked trying new things.'

It was true. Ryan had been adventurous—a trait that had initially drawn her to him and ultimately taken him away. The motorcycle accident had happened three weeks after their brief summer romance ended, before she'd even known she was pregnant. Sometimes when Jett smiled a certain way, she caught glimpses of Ryan's carefree spirit, a bittersweet reminder of what might have been.

Sarah had long ago made peace with raising Jett alone. Ryan's parents lived interstate and, although they sent birthday cards and the occasional Christmas gift, they'd never been actively involved in Jett's life. She'd built her own support system—friends like Elaine who had become Jett's unofficial grandmother, a small community of other single parents who understood the unique challenges and joys of raising children alone.

Still, watching Oliver interact so naturally with Jett had stirred something unexpected. Not regret, exactly, but a quiet wondering about what it might be like to share the journey of parenting with someone who cared.

'Excuse me, how much for the turquoise necklace?'

Sarah's head snapped up to find a customer examining her display. 'Thirty-five dollars,' she said, pushing thoughts of Oliver aside and pasting on her market-day smile. 'Or three pieces for ninety.'

As the afternoon progressed, the markets filled with families enjoying the balmy spring weather. Sarah kept busy with a steady stream of customers but found her eyes drifting to the entrance whenever a tall, dark-haired man appeared. It was a habit she couldn't seem to break, this hopeful scanning of crowds for a glimpse of Oliver Johnson.

'You're being ridiculous,' she told herself firmly as she made change for a customer. 'He's probably forgotten all about you.'

But Jett hadn't forgotten. Every market day

for months, he'd asked about the mango man at Dunmora.

'Can we go back to the Dunmora markets, Mummy?'

'We go to the Bargara Beach markets now, sweetie. They're closer to our home,' Sarah would remind him gently, not wanting to admit that she'd deliberately changed which markets they attended after Oliver never called. It had been too painful to keep setting up her stall at Dunmora, constantly watching for him, wondering if he'd appear with his mangoes and that shy smile that had made her stomach flip.

'Lookin' for someone?'

Sarah turned to find her market neighbour, Elaine, watching her with knowing eyes. The older woman sold homemade jams and had taken Sarah under her wing when she'd first started at the Bargara Beach markets two years ago.

'Just checking the crowd,' Sarah said lightly. 'Good turnout tonight.'

Elaine snorted. 'You've been watching that entrance like a hawk since you set up. That farmer boy from Dunmora never showed up here, then?'

Sarah felt herself flush. 'I'm not looking for anyone.'

'Course not,' Elaine agreed amiably. 'And I'm not seventy-three with arthritis.'

'He's just someone Jett liked,' Sarah insisted. 'He was good with kids.'

'Mmm-hmm.' Elaine began rearranging her jam jars. 'You know, my Tom was good with kids too. That's how I knew he'd make a good husband—fifty-six years we had together.'

Sarah rolled her eyes. 'I talked to the man for an afternoon, Elaine. I'm not planning our wedding.'

'More's the pity,' Elaine replied. 'A girl your age shouldn't be alone.'

'I'm not alone,' Sarah said, gesturing toward Jett, who was carefully counting change for a customer. 'I have excellent company.'

'You know what I mean.'

Sarah did know, but she also knew the reality of dating as a single mother. Most men lost interest the moment they learned about Jett, and the few who didn't usually faded away once they realised her son would always come first. She'd stopped dating entirely after the last disaster—a seemingly nice accountant who'd suggested that boarding school might be 'the best solution for everyone.'

Oliver had been different, though. He'd noticed Jett first, crouching down to her little boy's level to explain how the mango pattern varied with different varieties. He'd answered every one of Jett's rapid-fire questions with the same patience and attention he'd given to adult customers. It was only after Jett had wandered off to look at a nearby toy stall that Oliver had turned that thoughtful gaze on her.

'I figured when he didn't call, it was because of Jett,' Sarah admitted quietly. 'I thought he'd changed his mind about dating a woman with a child.'

A high-pitched squeal jolted Sarah from her memories. 'Mummy! Look, Kimmy's here!'

Sarah turned to see Jett waving frantically at his best friend from preschool, who was approaching with her parents. She smiled and waved, pushing thoughts of Oliver firmly aside. This was her life now—her son, her craft business, her friends. It was a good life, even if sometimes she found herself scanning crowds for a man who'd clearly forgotten her number as easily as he'd taken it.

***

The Bean Counter was busy when Oliver arrived, the lunch crowd still lingering over coffee and cake. He spotted Jessica immediately—her yellow dress bright against the café's muted decor, her blonde hair pulled back in a neat ponytail. She was pretty in a wholesome, approachable way, and she was checking her watch with a slight frown.

Oliver glanced at his own watch. Four-fifteen. Great start.

He made his way to her table, bumping into a chair and nearly upending a water glass in the process. 'Sorry I'm late,' he said as he reached her. 'Farm emergency.'

Jessica looked up with a smile that faltered slightly as she took him in. Was it the mud on his boots that he hadn't managed to completely clean off? Or perhaps the small grease stain on his jeans he'd only noticed in the car?

'Oliver?' she asked, a note of uncertainty in her voice.

'That's me,' he confirmed, sliding

awkwardly into the chair opposite her. 'You must be Jessica.'

Her smile returned, though not quite reaching her eyes. 'Yes! It's nice to finally meet you. Your messages were so lovely.'

Oliver made a mental note to kill Amelia slowly. 'Right. Thanks.'

An awkward silence descended. Jessica took a sip of her water, and Oliver found himself staring blankly at the menu, though he had no appetite whatsoever.

'So,' Jessica said brightly, 'you mentioned you've been experimenting with sourdough lately?'

Oliver blinked. 'Did I?'

'In your message yesterday,' she prompted. 'You said you'd finally mastered the perfect crust.'

'Ah.' Oliver cleared his throat. 'Right. Sourdough. It's . . .crusty.'

Jessica's smile dimmed slightly. 'Are you feeling alright?'

'Fine,' Oliver assured her. 'Just been a long morning on the farm. To be honest, my sister handles most of the baking. I pass the ingredients and I'm . . . um, the taste tester.'

Jessica laughed. 'Well, that's an important job too. I'm hopeless in the kitchen myself—except for cookies. I have to make those with my kindergarteners.'

A waitress appeared, and they ordered—a flat white for him, a chai latte for her.

'You're a kindergarten teacher?' Oliver asked, remembering Amelia's briefing.

Jessica's face lit up. 'Yes! I teach at Elliott Heads. I've just started a garden project with my class—we're growing vegetables and learning about plant life cycles. The children are so excited about it.'

Oliver nodded, genuinely interested. 'What are you growing?'

'Oh, all sorts! Lettuce, carrots, cherry tomatoes—things that grow quickly so the children can see results. We've just harvested our first radishes.'

'You should try sugar snap peas,' Oliver suggested, warming to the topic. 'They're fast-growing, and kids can eat them straight from the vine. My sister Amelia used to grow them when we were kids.'

Jessica beamed. 'That's a wonderful idea! Have you done much gardening with children?'

'Not really,' Oliver admitted. 'Just grew up on a farm.'

'Oh, yes, your profile mentioned you're a cane farmer. That must be fascinating work.'

Oliver relaxed slightly, on familiar ground at last. 'It has its moments. We've just finished the harvest season—the crush, we call it. Now we're preparing for next year's planting and maintaining the ratoon crop.'

Jessica listened attentively, but her attention wandered as he spoke. Farming wasn't her passion, despite the vegetable garden. Their drinks arrived, providing another welcome break in the conversation.

'So,' Jessica said after taking a sip of her chai, 'you mentioned you enjoy astronomy? Have you been to the observatory in Bundaberg?'

Oliver silently added another tally mark to Amelia's death sentence. 'Not recently,' he hedged. 'Been busy with the farm.'

'Oh, they have the most wonderful Friday night viewings at the observatory! They're focusing on the southern constellations tonight.' She paused, looking at him with a hopeful smile. 'Perhaps we could go sometime?'

Oliver shifted uncomfortably. 'I don't really get many nights off, to be honest.'

'I understand,' she said, though disappointment flickered across her face. 'Farming must keep you busy. What about the weekend markets? Your profile mentioned you enjoy them.'

'I do go to the markets,' Oliver said truthfully. 'I sell mangoes there when they're in season.'

'Oh, that sounds lovely! Are they in season now?'

'Just starting,' Oliver said, a plan forming in his mind. 'The early varieties are ripening.'

'Would you be at the Bargara night market tonight, then?' Jessica asked. 'We could walk around, maybe look at the stars afterward?'

'No, not tonight,' Oliver said, seizing the escape route. 'I need to get back to the farm. Lots of work to do before dark.'

'Oh.' Jessica's face fell. 'Some other time, perhaps?'

Oliver stared into his coffee, discomfort mingling with guilt. 'Look, Jessica, you seem really nice—'

'But there's not really a spark,' she finished for him, her smile tightening slightly. 'It's okay, Oliver. I've been on enough first dates to recognise when someone isn't interested.'

Oliver shifted awkwardly. 'I'm sorry.'

'Don't be.' She took another sip of her chai, her eyes studying him over the rim. 'Though I am curious—your messages were so enthusiastic about baking and astronomy, but you don't seem interested in them. Actually, not interested in much at all.'

'That obvious, huh?'

'You have an expressive face,' she said diplomatically. 'So, what parts of your profile are true?'

'I do farm sugar cane,' Oliver offered. 'And I sell mangoes at the markets when they're in season. That's about it.'

Jessica nodded thoughtfully. 'Well, I'm glad we've cleared the air.' She glanced at her watch. 'I should probably get going anyway.'

Relief mingled with a touch of regret as

Oliver realised Jessica was actually okay.

'Thanks for meeting me,' she said, gathering her purse. 'My car's just down the street.' She hesitated, then added with a warm smile, 'For what it's worth, you do seem perfectly nice, even without the sourdough expertise.'

Oliver managed a genuine smile in return. 'Thanks. And I meant what I said about the sugar snap peas. They really are good for kids' gardens.'

'I'll definitely try them,' Jessica promised. 'And if you're ever selling mangoes at the market, I'd love to buy some. We're studying tropical fruits next month.'

'I'll let you know,' Oliver said.

With a final smile, Jessica left, leaving Oliver to pay the bill and contemplate the damage Amelia had done to his reputation. Still, it hadn't been the disaster he'd feared. Jessica had been understanding, even kind, about the whole situation.

As he walked back to his ute, Oliver's thoughts drifted unexpectedly to Sarah. Would she be at the markets this weekend? It was early in the mango season, but some of his early varieties were ready. He could have brought a small selection, set up his usual stall—

'Don't be ridiculous,' he whispered to himself as he climbed into the driver's seat. 'She's probably left the district. Stop dreaming.'

Still, as he drove back toward the farm, Oliver found himself wondering if Sarah's son, Jett, that was his name, still remembered how to tell when a Kensington Pride was perfectly ripe. The boy had been a quick study, his small hands gentle on the fruit as Oliver showed him what to look for.

For the first time since agreeing to this coffee date, Oliver smiled. Maybe a trip to the markets wasn't a bad idea.

Chapter 4

'Can't see you, Grandmère,' Amelia said.

'Is this thing working? Hugo, is the camera on?' Grandmère's voice came through clearly, though the video showed only the ceiling of what appeared to be a French apartment.

'It's on, Margot, they just can't see us because you're holding it wrong,' came Papa's patient reply.

Oliver exchanged amused glances with Guy and Amelia as they sat clustered around the kitchen table, Amelia's laptop open before them. It was Sunday evening, and the promised weekly video call from France had finally connected after three failed attempts.

'Here, let me—' There was a rustling noise, followed by a dizzying spin of images before Grandmère's face appeared, far too close to the camera. Her eyes were magnified comically behind her reading glasses as she peered into the screen.

'Ah! There you are!' she exclaimed triumphantly. 'Can you see me too?'

'We can see your pores now, Grandmère,'

Amelia said with a laugh. 'Maybe move back a bit?'

Grandmère shifted, and the camera panned out to reveal her sitting in a sunny apartment, lace curtains billowing in a gentle breeze behind her. Papa sat beside her, looking relaxed in a pale blue linen shirt, his usual serious expression replaced by a contented smile. Their parents stood behind them, Mum's face glowing with excitement and, to Oliver's surprise, Dad wearing a beret.

'Is that a beret?' Guy asked incredulously, leaning forward.

Dad grinned sheepishly and touched the dark blue fabric. 'When in France,' he said with a shrug. 'Your mother says it suits me.'

'You look like an artist, Dad,' Amelia said diplomatically. 'Very . . . European.'

'It was my idea,' Grandmère announced proudly. 'Hugo needs to embrace his heritage!'

'How's France?' Oliver asked, steering the conversation away from his father's unexpected fashion choice. 'Have you seen the vineyards yet?'

'Oh, *mes petits choux*!' Grandmère clasped

her hands together, her face radiant. 'We arrived in Lyon yesterday, and tomorrow we go to my village. But already, it is *magnifique*! The food, the people, the buildings—everything is as beautiful as I remembered.'

'Your grandmother hasn't stopped smiling since we landed,' Papa said fondly, patting her hand. 'Even when we got lost trying to find the apartment.'

'We weren't lost,' Grandmère insisted. 'We were exploring.'

'We walked in circles for two hours,' Dad deadpanned, but his eyes twinkled with good humour. 'Carrying luggage.'

'Exercise is good for you, Hugo,' Grandmère said dismissively. 'And we found the most charming little bakery while we were . . . exploring.'

'The bread,' Mum interjected, leaning closer to the camera. 'You wouldn't believe the bread here. And the cheese! I've never tasted anything like it.'

Oliver was taken aback by the change in their usually reserved mother. Ellen Johnson was not given to exclamations or hyperbole, yet here she was, rhapsodising about cheese with shining eyes and flushed cheeks. France clearly agreed with her.

'Where are Charlotte and Greg?' Amelia asked, scanning the background with a frown.

'They've gone to Paris for the weekend,' Ellen explained. 'Charlotte wanted to see the Louvre, and there was a train. So—' She waved her hand vaguely, clearly having embraced the spontaneity of travel.

'Dad let them go off without a detailed itinerary?' Guy murmured to Oliver. 'Who is this man and what has he done with our father?'

Oliver stifled a laugh. Even when they were kids, their father's idea of a day trip to Bargara Beach had always involved military-level planning and multiple backup routes.

'And how are things at the farm?' Dad asked, making a visible effort to sound casual, though they all recognised the strain in his voice. Four days without checking on his crops was probably a personal record.

'Everything's fine, Dad,' Guy said reassuringly. 'The irrigation system on the east field is fixed, and I've scheduled the contractors for the fence repairs next week.'

Dad nodded, clearly fighting the urge to ask for more details. 'And the mangoes, Oli?'

'Coming along,' Oliver reported. 'The early varieties are starting to ripen. I'm thinking of taking some to the Bargara markets.'

'Oh, the markets!' Mum's face lit up further. 'Will you be seeing that lovely girl again? The one with the crafts?'

Oliver felt heat creep up his neck. 'I don't know. Maybe.' He studiously avoided looking at Amelia, who was surely grinning like the Cheshire cat beside him.

'What lovely girl?' Grandmère demanded, leaning closer to the camera again. 'Oliver has a girl?'

'Sarah,' Mum supplied helpfully. 'He met her at the markets last year. She makes jewellery and has the most adorable little boy. I bought some presents from her stall when Oliver was next to her at the Christmas markets. What was his name again, Oli?'

'Jett,' Oliver mumbled, cursing his mother's sudden onset of matchmaking across international borders. 'And I barely know her.

We talked once.'

'Why wasn't I told about this?' Grandmère's face filled the screen again. 'Once is enough when it's the right person,' Grandmère declared with the confidence of someone who'd been married for over sixty years.

Amelia snorted beside Oliver, and he frowned.

'Your grandfather proposed to me after one dance,' Grandmère said.

'And then courted you properly for two years before you actually got married,' Papa reminded her with a chuckle.

'Details,' Grandmère dismissed. 'The important thing is, he knew.'

'Speaking of dating,' Amelia interjected gleefully, 'Oliver went on his first online date yesterday!'

Oliver shot her a glare that would have withered the sugar cane, but it was too late. The damage was done.

'Online date?' Mum echoed, her expression a mixture of surprise and delight. 'Who with?'

'A kindergarten teacher named Jessica,' Amelia supplied before Oliver could stop her.

'Very pretty. Blonde. Teaches at Elliot Heads.'

'How did it go?' Dad asked, looking oddly proud. 'Did you take her somewhere nice?'

'I—' Oliver started, but Amelia cut him off again.

'Coffee at The Bean Counter,' she said. 'And it went—'

'Fine,' Oliver interrupted firmly. 'It went fine.'

'Oh, Oliver!' Mum clapped her hands together. 'I'm so pleased you're putting yourself out there.'

'About time,' Grandmère added. 'A man your age should be thinking about settling down.'

'I'm only twenty-five,' Oliver protested weakly.

'Exactly!' Grandmère nodded as if he'd made her point for her. 'When I was twenty-five, I already had your father.'

'Different times, Margot,' Papa said gently.

'The heart doesn't change with time,' Grandmère insisted. 'Now, tell me about this Jessica. Is she French?'

'No,' Oliver said shortly.

'Ah, well, no one is perfect,' Grandmère sighed. 'Will you see her again?'

'No,' Oliver repeated, wishing the floor would open and swallow him whole. 'It wasn't . . . We didn't . . . It just wasn't a match.'

'And that's fine!' Mum said encouragingly. 'The important thing is that you tried. There are plenty more fish in the sea.'

'Or on the internet,' Amelia added with a smirk.

Oliver briefly contemplated sororicide.

'Well, keep trying,' Dad said, in the same tone he used when discussing failed crop experiments. 'You'll find the right fertiliser mix eventually.'

Guy choked on his beer.

'Your father means the right person,' Mum translated hastily. 'Don't you, Hugo?'

'Of course,' Dad agreed. 'Though the principle is the same. Trial and error. Data collection. Eventual success.'

'I think what Dad's trying to say,' Guy said, still coughing slightly, 'is good luck.'

'Exactly,' Dad nodded firmly. 'Good luck with the . . . dating.'

The conversation mercifully moved on to other topics—Grandmère's cousins they would meet the next day, the excellent wine they'd tried at a local restaurant, and Papa's run-in with a particularly persistent street vendor. Oliver found his attention drifting, his thoughts wandering back to the markets and whether Sarah would be there on Friday.

'. . . don't you think, Oliver?' His mother's voice snapped him back to the present.

'Sorry, what?' he asked, blinking.

Ellen's eyes narrowed knowingly. 'I said, if Jessica wasn't the right match, perhaps you should look for this Sarah again.'

'I don't even know if she still lives in Bundaberg,' Oliver said, trying to sound disinterested. 'It's been a year.'

'You won't know until you look,' Mum pointed out reasonably. 'What have you got to lose?'

'His dignity,' Guy muttered under his breath.

Oliver kicked him under the table.

'Well, we should get going,' Dad said, glancing at his watch. 'We're meeting some of your grandmother's cousins for *un déjeuner décontracté*.'

Amelia stifled a laugh, and Oliver grinned at her. Dad's pronunciation was appalling.

'That means lunch,' Mum translated. 'Your father's been confusing the poor locals with his accent everywhere we go.'

'At least you're trying, Dad.' Oliver gave a thumbs-up in front of the screen.

'Call us again next Sunday,' Mum instructed. 'And Oliver, do let us know how the dating goes!'

After a flurry of goodbyes and Grandmère's solemn promise to find Oliver a nice French girl if all else failed, the call ended, leaving the three siblings sitting in silence.

'That went well,' Amelia said brightly.

'Why the hell did you tell them about my date with Jessica?' Oliver demanded.

'Because you weren't going to,' she replied, unrepentant. 'And they seemed happy about it.'

'Too happy,' Guy agreed. 'Did you see Dad? I thought he was going to start planning a wedding.'

'He compared dating to fertiliser,' Oliver

said flatly.

'Which, coming from Dad, is practically poetry,' Amelia pointed out. 'He was trying to be supportive.'

Oliver slumped back in his chair. 'Now they're all going to ask about my dating life every time we FaceTime.'

'Would that be so terrible?' Amelia asked, her tone gentler. 'They care about you, Oli.'

'Besides,' Guy added, standing up and stretching, 'at least it distracts Dad from interrogating us about the farm.' He headed for the door. 'I'm going to check the irrigation timers before bed.'

After he'd gone, Amelia turned to Oliver, her expression unusually serious. 'So, are you going to the markets at Dunmora on Friday?'

Oliver hesitated. 'I don't know. Maybe.'

'To look for Sarah?'

'To sell mangoes,' he insisted, though they both knew it wasn't the whole truth.

Amelia studied him for a moment, then nodded. 'Well, if you need help setting up your stall, let me know. I'm free. Myron is working all weekend.'

'Thanks,' Oliver said, surprised by the offer. 'I might take you up on that.'

Amelia smiled and closed her laptop. 'In the meantime, I've scheduled another date for you on Tuesday, anyway. Her name is Brittany, she's an accountant, and she loves action movies.'

'Amelia!' Oliver groaned.

'Just keeping my options open,' she said with a wink as she left the room.

Oliver sat alone at the kitchen table, contemplating the absurdity of his situation. A sister determined to find him love through the internet, a family cheering from across the world, and him still thinking about a woman he'd met once a year ago.

He'd go to the markets on Friday, he decided. Just to sell mangoes. And if Sarah happened to be there . . . well, he'd cross that bridge when he came to it.

***

'You should try it,' Elaine insisted, pushing another homemade jam scone across the table toward Sarah. 'Changed my life, it did.'

Sarah took the scone despite being already full from the first one. Saying no to Elaine was like trying to stop a tidal wave with a teaspoon—futile and likely to leave you soaked.

'Online dating is not going to change my life,' she said, taking a bite to be polite. 'It's just going to introduce me to a bunch of men who'll disappear the moment they find out I have a four-year-old.'

They were sitting in Elaine's cosy kitchen, the Sunday afternoon sunlight streaming through gingham curtains. Jett was in the garden with Elaine's grandson, Charlie, the two boys engrossed in a complex game involving dinosaurs and what appeared to be world domination.

'Not everyone's like that Richard,' Elaine said dismissively. 'Good riddance to bad rubbish, I say.'

Sarah smiled despite herself. Elaine had never forgiven 'that Richard' for suggesting boarding school for Jett. In Elaine's world, there were few sins greater than not appreciating children.

'Besides,' Elaine continued, pouring more tea, 'my niece met her husband online. Married two years now and expecting their first. And my hairdresser's daughter—'

'Found her soulmate on CountryConnections, I know,' Sarah finished for her. Elaine had been regaling her with online dating success stories for weeks now. 'But I'm not looking for a husband, Elaine. I'm perfectly happy as we are.'

'Course you are,' Elaine agreed readily. 'You and Jett make a lovely little family. But that doesn't mean you can't have more, does it? A partner. Someone to share the load.'

Sarah sighed, running a finger around the rim of her teacup. The truth was, she had considered it. Late at night, after Jett was asleep, when the house was quiet and the worry of being a sole parent pressed heavily in her mind—she'd thought about what it might be like to have someone to talk to, to laugh with, to help make decisions.

'I wouldn't even know where to start,' she admitted. 'What would I put in a profile? "Single mum, makes jewellery, comes with energetic four-year-old who asks a million questions a day"?'

'Sounds perfect to me,' Elaine said with a

nod. 'The right man would read that and think he'd hit the jackpot.'

Sarah laughed. 'You're an incurable romantic, Elaine Hargraves.'

'Married fifty-six years? Someone found me appealing.'

They watched the boys through the window for a moment, Jett's dark head bent close to Charlie's fair one as they arranged plastic dinosaurs in formation.

'He asks about him, you know,' Sarah said quietly. 'The mango farmer. Every market day.'

'Ah.' Elaine's expression softened. 'Children remember the oddest things.'

'It's not odd,' Sarah found herself defending Oliver. 'He was kind to Jett. And took an interest in what he was saying. That matters to him.'

Elaine's shrewd eyes studied her face. 'And to his mother, I'd wager.'

Sarah felt her cheeks warm. 'He was nice, that's all.'

'And yet here you are, a year later, still hoping he'll turn up with his mangoes.'

'I'm not—' Sarah began, then sighed. 'Am I that obvious?'

'Only to someone who's known you since you started at the markets when you were pregnant with Jett,' Elaine said gently. 'You scan every crowd, love. Your face falls a little each time he's not there.'

Sarah stared into her tea, embarrassed to be so transparent. 'It's ridiculous. We talked once, Elaine. A few hours.'

'Sometimes that's all it takes,' Elaine said. 'My Tom proposed after our first date.'

'Different times,' Sarah reminded her.

'The heart doesn't change with time,' Elaine countered. 'But chances do pass us by if we don't take them.'

Sarah knew what was coming next.

'Which is why,' Elaine continued, right on cue, 'you should try online dating. If this mango man doesn't show up, at least you'll have other options.'

Sarah ran her finger around the rim of her teacup. 'It's not that simple, Elaine. Most men aren't exactly lining up to date a woman with a child.'

'The right man wouldn't see Jett as an obstacle,' Elaine said firmly.

'That's what I thought about David last year, remember? Three dates in, he suggested Jett might be "happier in a structured environment". Code for "can the kid be somewhere else when I come over.".'

Elaine made a dismissive noise. 'David was a fool. Not all men are like that.'

'And not all men are like Ryan, either,' Sarah said quietly.

Elaine's expression softened at the mention of Jett's father. 'No, dear, they're not. Ryan was a special young man in many ways.'

'He would have been a good dad,' Sarah said, the familiar ache of what-might-have-been rising in her chest. 'If he'd had the chance.'

'I believe he would have,' Elaine agreed. 'But life had other plans.'

Through the window, they watched Jett, now orchestrating an elaborate dinosaur battle with Charlie. His animated gestures and infectious laugh were so reminiscent of Ryan that it sometimes took Sarah's breath away.

'It'll be five years next month,' Sarah said. 'Since the accident. Sometimes I wonder if I'm doing right by Jett, raising him without a father figure.'

'You're doing wonderfully,' Elaine assured her. 'That boy is happy, healthy, and confident. Ryan would be proud of you both.'

Sarah nodded, grateful for the reassurance. 'Jett's been asking more questions lately. Specific ones. What did his daddy's voice sound like? Did he like dinosaurs too? Questions I sometimes don't have answers for.'

'That's natural at his age,' Elaine said. 'He's making sense of his place in the world.'

'I've been thinking it might be time to visit Ryan's parents again,' Sarah admitted. 'They have videos, photos from when Ryan was young. Things that might help Jett connect with that part of himself.'

'That's a good idea,' Elaine approved. 'And speaking of connections...' She gestured meaningfully toward Sarah's laptop.

Sarah smiled despite herself. 'Back to the dating app, are we?'

'Just saying that moving forward doesn't mean leaving the past behind,' Elaine said wisely. 'It means building on the foundation you already have.'

Put that way, it didn't sound completely unreasonable. And what did she have to lose? If nothing else, it might help her finally stop looking for Oliver in every crowd.

'I'll think about it,' Sarah promised, knowing it would be easier than arguing.

'Put that way, it didn't sound completely unreasonable. And what did she have to lose? If nothing else, it might help her finally stop looking for Oliver in every crowd.

'I'll think about it,' Sarah promised, knowing it would be easier than arguing.

Elaine beamed in triumph. 'That's all I ask. Now, have another scone. You're skin and bones, girl!'

Chapter 5

'You can't wear that.'

Oliver looked down at his faded blue work shirt and relatively clean jeans. 'What's wrong with this?'

Amelia rolled her eyes so dramatically that Oliver worried they might get stuck that way. 'You're going to the cinema, not mending fences. Don't you own any clothes that don't scream "I've been wrestling with agricultural equipment all day"?'

'I like this shirt,' Oliver protested. 'And I have been wrestling with agricultural equipment all day.'

They were standing in Oliver's bedroom, the late afternoon sun slanting through the shutters. Outside, the humidity hung heavy in the air, promising rain later. Oliver had been hoping the weather might provide an excuse to cancel tonight's date, but the downpour had yet to materialise, and Amelia had been monitoring his movements with the vigilance of a prison guard since lunch.

Ten days had passed since the coffee date

with Jessica. That hadn't gone well, though at least they'd parted on friendly terms. But Amelia had wasted no time in setting up this second date for Thursday evening, giving him just enough time to recover from the first disaster before launching him into another.

'At least wear the green button-down,' she insisted, rummaging through his wardrobe. 'The one Charlotte got you for Christmas.'

'It's too hot for that.'

'It's too hot for excuses, Oli. Brittany is an accountant—a professional. You can't turn up looking like you've just fallen off a tractor.'

'I haven't fallen off a tractor since I was twelve,' Oliver muttered, but he took the green shirt she was now brandishing at him like a weapon.

Guy appeared in the doorway, leaning against the frame with a barely concealed smirk. 'Having a fashion crisis, brother?'

'I'm having a sister crisis,' Oliver replied. 'Didn't you have something to fix in the shed?'

'Nope. Everything's running smoothly.' Guy's smirk widened. 'Unlike your love life.'

'It's not a love life,' Oliver protested,

shrugging off his work shirt. 'It's a hostage situation.'

Amelia huffed. 'You should be thanking me. Brittany is perfect for you. She's practical, organised, and she loves the outdoors.'

'She's an accountant,' Oliver pointed out, buttoning up the green shirt. 'How much time does she actually spend outdoors?'

'She goes hiking on weekends,' Amelia said. 'At least, that's what her profile claims.'

'That fills me with confidence.'

Guy chuckled. 'Maybe she'll help you organise the farm books. Heaven knows they could use it.'

'There's nothing wrong with my bookkeeping,' Oliver growled, tucking in his shirt and checking his reflection in the mirror. The green did bring out his eyes, though he'd never admit that to Charlotte or Amelia.

'There's nothing wrong with your bookkeeping because I do it all,' Guy corrected. 'Your idea of financial records is a shoebox full of receipts.'

'It's a system.'

'It's a fire hazard.'

'Boys,' Amelia interrupted, 'can we focus? Oli, you need to leave in ten minutes if you're going to make it to Bundaberg by seven. Brittany said she'd meet you in the cinema foyer.'

Oliver nodded, trying to ignore the knot of dread in his stomach. One more date. He could survive one more date. And then maybe Amelia would leave him alone long enough for him to focus on the Bargara market. If the weather held, he'd take his early mangoes and set up his usual stall.

'You look good. She'll love you,' Amelia said, her tone softening as she brushed imaginary lint from his shoulder. 'Just try to relax and be yourself.'

'My self wants to stay home and check the irrigation system before the rain hits,' Oliver said.

'I've got the irrigation covered,' Guy assured him. 'And the rest of the farm. Go watch a movie, eat some overpriced popcorn, talk to a woman who isn't related to you by blood.'

'A novel concept,' Amelia agreed. 'Now go. And remember—'

'No talking about sugar cane prices,

irrigation systems, or the latest tractor models,' Oliver recited dutifully. 'I've got it.'

'And no checking your watch every five minutes,' Amelia added.

'And maybe try smiling,' Guy suggested. 'People generally find that less terrifying than your usual expression.'

Oliver scowled at him. 'This is my smiling face.'

'God help us all,' Guy muttered.

Ten minutes later, Oliver was in his ute, driving toward Bundaberg with a sense of impending doom. The sky was darkening with both the setting sun and gathering storm clouds, and the air felt thick with electricity. Perfect weather for a movie, he supposed, if not for the drive home afterwards.

He tried to remember what Amelia had told him about Brittany. Thirty-two, divorced, no children, worked for an accounting firm in Bundaberg. Liked hiking, cooking, and action movies—the last being the only detail that had given Oliver any hope for the evening.

By the time he reached the cinema, the first fat drops of rain were beginning to fall. He parked as close as he could manage and jogged to the entrance, grateful at least for the excuse to keep the date short. 'Sorry, need to get home before the roads flood' seemed like a perfectly reasonable escape strategy.

Brittany was waiting in the lobby, checking her phone with a slight frown. She was attractive in a polished way—sleek brown hair cut in a bob, subtle makeup, wearing a stylish blouse and tailored trousers that made Oliver suddenly conscious of his farm-boy attire despite the green shirt upgrade.

'Brittany?' he approached with what he hoped was a normal, non-terrifying smile.

She looked up, her frown instantly transforming into a bright smile. 'Oliver! Hi!' She tucked her phone into a small leather handbag. 'I was beginning to think I'd been stood up.'

Oliver checked his watch. He was three minutes late. 'Sorry about that. Traffic.'

'No worries,' she said breezily. 'Shall we get tickets? There's a new rom-com showing that's supposed to be amazing. It's got that actor from the TV show about the hospital—you know the one?'

Oliver didn't know the one, but he nodded anyway. 'Actually, I thought maybe that new action film might be good? The one with the explosions?' He gestured vaguely toward a poster featuring a man leaping from a burning building.

Brittany's smile dimmed slightly. 'Oh. I'd heard the plot was a bit—thin.'

'Explosions don't need much plot,' Oliver offered, then immediately regretted it as Brittany's eyebrows rose.

'I see,' she said, in a tone that suggested she did indeed see, and was not impressed. 'Well, there's a comedy showing too. About a family road trip gone wrong?'

Oliver seized on the compromise. 'Perfect. Comedy works.'

As they got in line for tickets, Oliver's phone buzzed in his pocket. He pulled it out to see a text from Guy.

Eastern irrigation system acting up. Nothing urgent. Enjoy your date.

Oliver frowned, quickly typing back: **Define 'up.**

The reply came seconds later: **Just making noise. I'll check it tomorrow.**

'Everything okay?' Brittany asked as they reached the ticket counter.

'Fine,' Oliver said, tucking his phone away. 'Just farm stuff.'

'Two for *Family Vacation Disaster*, please,' Brittany told the cashier, reaching for her purse.

'I've got it,' Oliver said quickly, handing over his card. One thing his mother had drilled into him was that the person who does the inviting does the paying, and while technically Amelia had done the inviting, he wasn't about to start the evening by letting Brittany pay.

'Thanks,' she said, seeming genuinely pleased. 'Shall we get popcorn?'

Oliver nodded, relieved to have successfully navigated the first hurdle. Maybe this wouldn't be as awkward as the coffee date with Jessica.

The concession line was long, giving them their first real opportunity to talk. Brittany seemed content to lead the conversation, telling him about her job at the accounting firm and a hiking trip she'd taken to Lamington National Park the previous month.

'Do you hike much?' she asked, finally opening a space for him to contribute.

'Not recreationally,' Oliver admitted. 'I do plenty of walking on the farm, but it's usually with a purpose.'

'Like what?'

'Checking irrigation lines, inspecting crops, mending fences—that sort of thing.'

Brittany nodded politely. 'Your profile mentioned you grow sugar cane? That must be interesting.'

Oliver hesitated, remembering Amelia's warning about talking farming. 'It has its moments.'

His phone buzzed again before he could elaborate. Another text from Guy: **Eastern irrigation system definitely making weird noise. Kind of a grinding sound. Still not urgent.**

Oliver frowned. Guy knew irrigation systems. If he said it wasn't urgent, it probably wasn't. But a grinding sound usually meant something needed attention before it became a bigger problem.

'Sorry,' he said, tucking the phone away again as they reached the counter. 'What size popcorn would you like?'

'Medium is fine. With butter, please.'

They collected their popcorn and drinks and found their seats just as the previews were starting. The theatre was about half full, mostly with couples and a few groups of teenagers. Oliver settled in, hoping the film would be at least moderately entertaining.

It wasn't.

Family Vacation Disaster turned out to be an aptly named film, though not in the way the creators had intended. The jokes fell flat, the acting was stiff, and the plot—involving a family getting lost in the woods with a series of increasingly implausible mishaps—made Oliver wonder if the scriptwriter had ever actually been camping.

Beside him, Brittany seemed equally unimpressed, picking at her popcorn without much enthusiasm. Oliver was just considering how to diplomatically suggest they cut their losses and leave when his phone vibrated again.

Eastern irrigation system now making serious noise. Like an angry bull. May need parts from town tomorrow.

Oliver grimaced. The eastern irrigation system controlled water flow to nearly a quarter of their fields. If it failed, they'd lose valuable watering time during a critical growth period. His phone buzzed again:

Don't panic. Not urgent tonight. Elena from the seasonal crew is helping. She's worked on similar systems in Brazil. Seriously, enjoy your date.

Then a third message: **Sorry for all the texts. Will stop now.**

Oliver stared at the message, momentarily distracted from his date disaster. Elena Santiago was the new hire who'd joined their seasonal crew three weeks ago—quiet, efficient, and, according to the supervisor, knowledgeable beyond her pay grade. Guy had mentioned her twice at dinner last week, which was unusual for his brother, who rarely noticed the seasonal workers beyond their productivity metrics.

He typed back quickly: **You called in seasonal help on a Thursday night?**

Guy's response came immediately: She was already at the farm, going over some water conservation proposals with me. Just happened to be here when the system started acting up.

Oliver raised an eyebrow at that. Guy reviewing proposals with a seasonal worker on a Thursday evening? That was certainly new. He slipped the phone back into his pocket, trying to refocus on the movie. On screen, the family's father was now attempting to build a shelter using twigs and what appeared to be the son's hoodie.

'That would collapse immediately,' Oliver muttered.

Brittany leaned closer. 'What?'

'That shelter. The structure's all wrong. You need a proper framework if you're going to use fabric as a cover.'

'Have you built many shelters?' she whispered back, seeming genuinely curious.

'A few,' Oliver admitted. 'When we were kids, Guy and I used to camp out near the creek. Built some pretty impressive structures over the years.'

Brittany smiled, the first genuine one he'd seen from her. 'That sounds nice. I was an only child, so I missed out on that kind of thing.'

For a moment, Oliver felt a connection—a tiny bridge forming across the chasm of awkwardness between them.

Then his phone buzzed again.

And again.

And a third time in quick succession.

'Sorry,' he murmured, pulling it out to check the screen.

Irrigation system now screaming like banshee. May have underestimated issue. Water spraying everywhere. Turned off main valve. Could use a hand when you're free. No rush. Actually, maybe some rush.

'Everything okay?' Brittany asked, obviously noting his expression.

'Farm emergency,' Oliver said apologetically. 'I might need to step out and make a call.'

'Oh.' Her disappointment was palpable. 'Sure.'

Oliver edged past the other patrons in their row, mumbling apologies as he accidentally stepped on someone's foot, and hurried to the lobby. He called Guy immediately.

'Tell me you didn't flood the eastern field,' he said as soon as Guy answered.

'I didn't flood the eastern field,' Guy replied, then added, 'I may have partially flooded the access road to the eastern field.'

Oliver closed his eyes briefly. 'How bad?'

'Not catastrophic. But the irrigation system housing has a crack, and when we tried to adjust the pressure, it—ah—expressed its displeasure forcefully.'

'I'm coming home.'

'No, don't,' Guy protested. 'I've got it under control now. I shut off the main valve and diverted the water flow. It'll hold until morning.'

'You sure?'

'Positive. Finish your date. I'm sorry I bothered you.'

Oliver glanced back toward the theatre doors. He should go back in. Abandoning Brittany halfway through the movie would be rude, even if the film was terrible. But the thought of sitting through another hour of bad jokes and implausible camping scenarios felt suddenly insurmountable.

'I'll be home in forty minutes,' he decided.

'Oli, don't—'

'It's fine. The date wasn't going great anyway.'

'Did you talk about irrigation systems?' Guy asked, a smile evident in his voice despite the crisis.

'No, I did not,' Oliver said indignantly. 'But the movie is terrible, and we have nothing in common, and now I have an actual legitimate reason to leave early.'

'Amelia's going to kill you.'

'I'll take my chances.'

Oliver ended the call and headed back into the theatre, sliding past the now-irritated row of viewers to reach his seat.

'Everything okay?' Brittany whispered as he sat down.

'Actually, there's a bit of a situation at the farm,' he said quietly. 'Our irrigation system has failed, and there's some flooding. I might need to head back soon.'

Brittany's face fell. 'Oh. That's inconvenient.'

'I'm really sorry,' Oliver said, and he meant it. Brittany seemed nice enough, even if there was no spark between them. 'I can drive you home first, of course.'

'That's all right,' she said, her tone cooler now. 'I drove myself. You should go if you need to.'

'I'll just stay until this scene ends,' Oliver offered, gesturing to the screen where the family was now attempting to fish using the mother's knitting wool. 'No need to rush out this second.'

Brittany nodded, turning her attention back to the movie. The awkwardness between them had returned tenfold, settling around them like a heavy blanket.

By the time the scene ended—with a predictable punchline involving the father falling into the creek—Oliver was itching to leave. He'd be lucky if the rain hadn't turned the access road into a complete mud pit by the time he got home.

'I should go,' he whispered. 'I really am sorry about this.'

'It's fine,' Brittany said, though her expression suggested it was anything but. 'Farming emergencies happen, I guess.'

'I'll get you more popcorn before I go,' Oliver offered, noting her nearly empty container. 'As an apology.'

Before she could protest, he had taken her popcorn bucket and was edging back down the row, desperate for any excuse to leave the stifling theatre.

In the lobby, he joined the short concession line, checking his phone while he waited. No new texts from Guy, which he hoped meant the situation hadn't deteriorated further.

'Medium popcorn with butter?' The attendant at the counter was young and friendly, with a shaggy haircut and an easy smile.

'Yes, thanks,' Oliver said, handing over his card.

As the attendant prepared the popcorn, Oliver glanced back toward the theatre entrance, mentally calculating how quickly he could deliver the snack and make his escape. When he turned back, he noticed the attendant had added extra butter without being asked.

'On the house,' the young man said with a wink. 'For the pretty lady in the green blouse. I noticed when you guys came in earlier.'

Oliver blinked, taken aback. 'Right. Thanks.'

He took the popcorn and headed back into the theatre, where the dim lighting made navigation challenging. As he reached their row, he could see Brittany's silhouette, but she seemed to be looking at something on her phone rather than the screen. The blue light illuminated her face, and Oliver could swear she was smiling more genuinely than she had all evening.

He edged past the other patrons again, balancing the popcorn carefully, until he reached their seats. As he sat down, Brittany hurriedly tucked her phone away, that same small smile lingering on her lips.

'One popcorn, extra butter apparently,' Oliver said, holding out the container.

'Oh, thank you!' Brittany reached for it just as Oliver's phone buzzed again in his pocket.

The movement of checking his phone while simultaneously passing the popcorn created a perfect storm of clumsiness. The popcorn bucket tilted, and before either of them could react, a cascade of buttery kernels poured directly into Brittany's lap and the bag she was holding there.

'Oh my God!' she gasped, loud enough that several nearby viewers turned to look.

'I'm so sorry!' Oliver whispered frantically, reaching to help but only managing to push more popcorn into the leather bag. 'I didn't mean to—'

'It's fine,' Brittany hissed, though her expression suggested it was very much not fine. 'Just... stop touching it.'

She stood abruptly, clutching her popcorn-filled purse, and shuffled past the other viewers toward the aisle. Oliver followed, acutely aware of the trail of kernels they were leaving and the disapproving murmurs around them.

In the lobby, Brittany was already tipping popcorn out of her purse into a trash can, her movements sharp with irritation.

'I am so sorry,' Oliver said again, hovering uselessly nearby. 'I can help clean—'

'I've got it,' she said curtly. 'You should go deal with your farm emergency.'

'At least let me—'

'Oliver,' Brittany interrupted, looking up with a tight smile, 'it's okay. Really. These things happen. But I think we both know this isn't... working.'

Oliver nodded, relief mingling with guilt.

'I'm sorry about the movie. And the popcorn. And the irrigation system.'

'It's fine,' she repeated, her tone softening slightly. 'We tried. Sometimes that's all you can do.' She paused, then added, 'For what it's worth, I think we would have figured out we're not compatible even without the agricultural emergency.'

'Probably,' Oliver agreed. 'You seem nice, though. And the popcorn guy thinks you're pretty.'

Brittany's eyebrows rose, but a small, genuine smile tugged at her lips. 'The one with the shaggy hair?'

'That's the one. He gave you extra butter.'

She laughed, the sound surprisingly warm after the tension of the last few minutes. 'Good to know.'

'So . . . I'll go, then,' Oliver said, gesturing vaguely toward the exit.

'Good luck with your irrigation system,' Brittany replied, and he couldn't tell if she was being sarcastic or sincere.

Either way, as Oliver stepped out into the now-steady rain, he felt lighter than he had all evening. He'd survived another date. Barely. And now he could focus on what really mattered—fixing the irrigation system and, hopefully, making it to the Bargara market in a couple of weeks.

The drive home was slower than usual, the rain creating sheets of water on the highway that reflected his headlights back at him. By the time he reached the farm, the dirt access road was indeed turning into mud, and he had to concentrate to keep the ute from sliding as he navigated toward the house.

The driveway was crowded with Guy's truck, and beside it, a beat-up blue sedan Oliver didn't recognise. As he splashed his way up the steps, he noticed Guy wasn't alone. A woman sat in the shadows of the porch swing, long dark hair pulled back in a practical braid, hands wrapped around her own steaming mug.

'That was fast,' Guy called as Oliver approached. 'How'd it go?'

'I dumped an entire bucket of popcorn in her lap,' Oliver replied flatly. 'Filled her handbag with melted butter.'

Guy stared at him for a moment, then burst

into laughter. 'You didn't.'

'I absolutely did.'

'Smooth operator.'

'Shut up and don't tell Amelia. How's the irrigation system?' Oliver asked, glancing toward the woman who had risen from the swing.

'Stabilised for now,' she said, stepping into the porch light. 'But you'll need to replace the housing and recalibrate the pressure valve. I've seen this issue on the sugar plantations in Brazil.'

'Oliver, this is Elena Santiago,' Guy introduced, a new warmth in his voice that Oliver hadn't heard before. 'She's been helping with the eastern quadrant irrigation.'

'Among other things,' Elena added with a small smile directed at Guy. She was striking rather than conventionally pretty, with intelligent eyes and the sun-weathered complexion of someone who lived outdoors. Something in the way she carried herself spoke of competence and experience beyond her years, which Oliver guessed to be around thirty.

'We appreciate the help,' Oliver said sincerely, shaking her offered hand. 'Especially on a Thursday night.'

'I was already here,' she explained. 'Your brother was showing me some of your sustainability initiatives. My family's farm in Brazil faces similar water conservation challenges.'

'Family farm?' Oliver questioned, glancing at Guy, who seemed unusually interested in the contents of his mug.

'Five generations,' Elena nodded. 'Though I've been travelling, learning different agricultural methods for the past three years. Australia is my final stop before heading home to implement what I've learned.'

'Elena has some innovative ideas for our irrigation system,' Guy said, finally looking up. 'I think Dad would be interested when he gets back.'

Something in Guy's expression—a rare animation, a certain tension around his eyes—caught Oliver's attention. His quiet, spreadsheet-focused brother seemed different in Elena's presence, more engaged, almost vibrant.

'I won't keep you,' Elena said, placing her mug on the small table. 'The rain is letting up, and I should get back to my rental.'

'I'll walk you to your car,' Guy offered immediately.

'No need to get more soaked,' she protested.

'I insist,' Guy said firmly. 'The driveway's treacherous when it's this wet.'

Oliver watched from the porch as Guy escorted Elena to her car, holding an umbrella over her though the rain had indeed slowed to a drizzle. They paused at her door, exchanging words he couldn't hear, but the way Guy leaned in slightly, the way Elena's hand briefly touched his arm—these small gestures spoke volumes.

When Guy returned to the porch, Oliver raised an eyebrow but said nothing.

'What?' Guy challenged, a defensive edge to his voice.

'Nothing,' Oliver replied innocently. 'Just never seen you voluntarily stand in the rain before.'

'She's been helpful with the irrigation planning,' Guy said stiffly. 'Professional courtesy.'

'Of course,' Oliver nodded solemnly. 'Very professional of you to review sustainability initiatives at nine p.m. on a Thursday.'

Guy's expression closed like a shutter. 'Some of us take the farm's future seriously.' He turned toward the door. 'I've got the system diagram laid out on the kitchen table.'

As they headed inside, Oliver cast one last glance at the retreating taillights of Elena's car. His brother had always been the steady one, the predictable one. But tonight, he'd glimpsed something else in Guy—a restlessness that had nothing to do with spreadsheets or irrigation systems.

Chapter 6

Sarah sat cross-legged on her couch, laptop balanced precariously on a throw pillow, the afternoon sun streaming through her living room windows. She'd been staring at the dating profile for twenty minutes, cursor hovering over the bright green 'Activate Profile' button.

'This is ridiculous,' she muttered, pushing a strand of hair behind her ear. 'It's just a dating profile, not a binding contract.'

She'd filled out the questionnaire honestly, chosen photos that weren't too staged or filtered—a candid one from her sister's wedding, another hiking with Jett in a carrier, and one from a night out with Elaine where she was laughing genuinely. The 'About Me' section had taken three drafts, but she'd finally settled on something that felt true without oversharing.

Creating a profile wouldn't mean she had to actually meet anyone, she reasoned. She could just browse, see what was out there. Maybe Elaine was right—maybe it would help her move on from this strange fixation on a man she barely knew.

With a deep breath, she clicked 'Sign Up' and began filling in the fields.

Name: Sarah Matthews Age: 24 Occupation: Jewellery Designer/Market Vendor Location: Bargara, Queensland

She paused at 'About Me,' her cursor blinking in the empty text box. How did one sum up their life in a paragraph? After several false starts, she typed:

Creative single mum with a passion for handcrafted jewellery and beach walks. My four-year-old son and I are a package deal—he's curious, energetic, and the centre of my world. Looking for someone kind, genuine, and patient who enjoys simple pleasures and doesn't mind the occasional dinosaur invasion.

It was honest, at least. No point in hiding Jett—he was non-negotiable. There was no need to say that Jett's father had died in a motorbike accident before she'd even known she was pregnant.

An image of Oliver flashed through her mind—his easy smile, the way he'd looked at her as if really seeing her, how his hands had moved with such care as he'd explained the different mango varieties.

'Stop it,' she scolded herself. 'Three hours of conversation a year ago does not a relationship make.'

She'd replayed their farmers' market meeting so many times it had taken on a mythic quality in her mind. What kind of person fixated on such a brief encounter? She sighed, knowing exactly what Elaine would say: that her subconscious was latching onto the memory of connection because she'd been depriving herself of social interaction outside of motherhood and work.

Maybe Elaine was right. Maybe having someone to share the load would make everything easier. Someone to laugh with after Jett went to bed, someone who might love her son almost as much as she did.

Sarah uploaded a recent photo of herself at the markets, smiling beside her jewellery display, and then sat back, her finger hovering over the 'Create Profile' button.

'Just to look,' she told herself firmly. 'Just to see what's out there.'

With a small surge of something like

courage, she clicked the button, then closed her laptop before she could change her mind.

Her phone immediately buzzed. Then again. And a third time in quick succession.

Three notifications from CountryConnections. Three men had already expressed interest in her profile. Her stomach fluttered with a mixture of flattery and discomfort.

She opened the first one and immediately grimaced. The message simply said, 'Ur hot. Dinner?' The profile picture showed a shirtless man flexing in a gym mirror.

The second wasn't much better: 'Single moms are my specialty 😉 '

'Gross,' Sarah muttered, nearly ready to deactivate her account immediately.

The third message was more polite, asking about her business and mentioning that he too enjoyed farmers' markets, but something about the professional headshot and carefully curated profile felt staged.

Sarah set her phone down, discouraged but determined. Elaine had warned her there would be plenty of frogs before any princes. This was just part of the process.

'I'll give it a week,' she decided. 'If they're all like this, I'm out.'

Closing her eyes, she tried to imagine a future with someone new, someone who could become important to both her and Jett. But frustratingly, the only face that came to mind was Oliver's, a man she barely knew and would probably never see again.

Outside, the moon cast silver light over her small garden, illuminating the mango tree she'd planted last year after Jett had become enchanted with the fruit. It hadn't yet produced anything, but it was growing steadily, its glossy leaves reaching toward the Queensland sky.

Much like her, Sarah thought—a work in progress, slowly putting down roots, waiting for the right time to bloom.

***

A week later.

'Hand me that wrench, would you?'

Oliver reached out a mud-covered hand without looking up from the mess of broken piping. The irrigation system had chosen a Sunday of all days to fail spectacularly, sending a geyser of water shooting ten feet into the air before Guy had managed to shut off the main valve.

Guy slapped the tool into Oliver's palm. 'You know, most people spend their Saturdays relaxing, maybe seeing friends, going on dates.'

'Most people aren't trying to run a sustainable farm,' Oliver grunted as he tightened a fitting. 'Almost got it.'

The sun beat down on them as they worked, both men covered in a mixture of sweat and soil. The eastern field still needed to be prepped for the late summer planting, the greenhouse required maintenance, and the local newspaper reported farmers' market attendance across the district had dropped slightly in the past few weeks.. The tourists were keeping the numbers up at the Bargara Beach markets, though.

Oliver straightened up, wiping his brow with his forearm, only succeeding in smearing more mud across his face. 'There. That should hold until we can get the replacement parts tomorrow. If we FaceTime with the olds tonight, we won't mention the pump or the irrigation failures to Dad.'

Guy nodded, then checked his phone. 'Amelia messaged: lunch is ready. And she says—and I quote— 'Tell Oliver to wash up properly this time. I'm not having mud all over my dining room chairs again.''

Oliver chuckled. '*Her* dining room chairs. Mum'd love to hear that.'

They reached the porch, where they dutifully removed their boots and hosed off the worst of the mud. The farmhouse kitchen was warm and fragrant with the smell of homemade bread and vegetable soup. Amelia jumped straight in.

'Look at this one, Oli.'

'This one's special. She makes her own pasta and has the most genuine smile I've seen on that entire app.' Amelia's eyes sparkled with mischief as she handed him the tablet.

Oliver rolled his eyes and reached for the soup ladle.

'She just joined today,' Amelia added casually. 'Seems like the universe is sending you a sign.'

Oliver handed the tablet back. 'The universe is sending me a sign that I need to pick some mangoes before it rains tomorrow.'

'You're impossible,' Amelia sighed, but with affection rather than genuine frustration. 'One of these days, Oliver Johnson, you're going to realise there's more to life than mangoes and irrigation systems.'

'Anyway, you're meeting her for dinner on Wednesday night.' Amelia smirked.

'What!'

The tablet rang, and Amelia shook her head. 'Can't talk now. France is calling.' She answered the call.

'Hi Grandmère.'

Chapter 7

Oliver tugged at his collar for the fifth time in as many minutes, feeling the stiff fabric scratch against his neck. The pale blue dress shirt—his only dress shirt—felt foreign against his skin, accustomed as he was to soft cotton T-shirts and flannel. He'd ironed it himself that afternoon, a task that had taken three attempts and left a suspicious brown mark on the ironing board that Amelia would definitely notice later.

The restaurant, *Maison Azure*, glowed with ambient lighting that somehow made everything look expensive. Crystal glasses caught the light, white tablecloths stretched pristine across each table, and waiters moved quietly between diners. Oliver felt distinctly out of place.

But there was Danielle—his third date—waving from a corner table, looking exactly like her profile picture—sleek dark hair, confident smile, impeccably dressed in what Oliver assumed was the kind of outfit featured in the magazines Lisette always brought home.

'Hello, Oliver. Lovely name, by the way. Very sophisticated. You found the place okay?'

Danielle asked as he approached, her smile warm and inviting.

'GPS is a wonderful thing,' Oliver replied, attempting to slide smoothly into his chair but catching the sleeve of his shirt on the back. He recovered with what he hoped was casual grace but suspected he looked more like a clunky fool.

'I hope you don't mind I went ahead and ordered wine,' she said, gesturing to the bottle. 'The Cabernet here is excellent.'

Oliver nodded appreciatively, though his wine knowledge extended about as far as "red" and "white." He accepted a glass, secretly wishing for a cold beer instead.

'You clean up nice,' Danielle said, her eyes appraising him. 'Very different from your profile pictures.'

'Farms and fancy clothes don't mix well,' he admitted. 'This shirt spends most of its life in the back of my closet.'

'Well, it should come out more often.' She smiled, and Oliver briefly felt a flicker of something. Not quite chemistry, but potential.

Maybe.

The waiter arrived with menus, launching

into a detailed description of specials that involved reductions and infusions and several ingredients Oliver couldn't pronounce. He nodded as if he understood completely.

'So, tell me more about your farm,' Danielle prompted after they ordered. 'It sounds fascinating.'

This was comfortable territory. Oliver relaxed slightly, describing the seasonal rhythms, the satisfaction of growing his mangoes from seed to harvest, the challenges and rewards. Danielle seemed genuinely interested, asking thoughtful questions about sustainability practices and heirloom varieties.

'It's not just a job,' he concluded. 'It's a way of life.'

'I can tell,' she said. 'Your whole face lights up when you talk about it.'

Their appetisers arrived—an artistic arrangement of something the menu had described as "deconstructed." Oliver surveyed the plate, trying to determine the strategy for eating it. Danielle began confidently, so he followed her lead.

'And what about you?' he asked. 'You

mentioned working in urban development?'

Danielle nodded enthusiastically. 'Yes, I help design mixed-use spaces in cities. The goal is creating communities where people can live, work, and play without relying on cars.'

'In Bundaberg?'

'No, I work remotely. Brisbane, Perth, Sydney. I've finished a few projects this year.'

'That's important work,' Oliver said, meaning it. 'We need more walkable communities.'

'Exactly! My dream project would be revitalising a downtown area. Something big, like Chicago or San Francisco.' Her eyes lit up as she continued, 'Actually, I just applied for a position with a firm in Seattle. It would be a huge opportunity.'

'Seattle? That's a long way away,' Oliver said, trying to keep his tone neutral.

'That's the exciting part,' Danielle continued. 'I've always wanted to live in a major metropolitan area. The energy, the culture, the constant innovation.' She leaned forward. 'Don't you ever feel that pull? To experience something completely different?'

Before Oliver could answer, their main courses arrived. His plate featured a carefully arranged piece of fish surrounded by colourful dots of sauce and what appeared to be vegetables cut into perfect cubes. The bright colour of one particular garnish caught his eye—a small pepper. He'd tried growing them a couple of years back, but hadn't seen quite that colour. He stared at it.

'So? Do you?'

He looked up apologetically. 'Sorry, I was looking at the colour of that pepper. Do I what?'

Danielle's expression changed, and held a little bit of exasperation. 'Feel the pull to experience something completely different? The vibrancy of a huge city?'

'Sometimes I think about trying new places,' he said diplomatically, picking up his fork. 'But the farm is pretty rooted, literally and figuratively.'

Danielle nodded, but her enthusiasm had dimmed slightly. 'I suppose we're opposites in that way. I get restless staying in one place too long.'

Oliver speared a bite of fish along with what

he assumed was the pretty coloured pepper garnish and popped it into his mouth. The flavours mingled pleasantly for approximately two seconds before the heat hit—a scorching, intense burn that spread across his tongue and down his throat. Not a sweet pepper. Definitely not sweet.

His eyes widened in panic as he reached for his water glass, draining it in one desperate gulp. The heat intensified, bringing tears to his eyes.

'Are you okay?' Danielle asked, concern etching her features.

Oliver nodded frantically, unable to speak, reaching for her water glass too, which she pushed toward him without hesitation. It wasn't enough. The inferno raged on.

With watering eyes and what little dignity he had left rapidly evaporating, he grabbed the water pitcher from the neighbouring empty table and drank directly from it, water dribbling down his chin and onto his only dress shirt.

'Oh my God,' Danielle whispered, half-concerned, half-mortified as nearby diners turned to stare.

'Sorry,' Oliver finally managed to gasp,

setting down the now-empty pitcher. 'Not . . . good with . . .spicy food.'

A waiter hurried over with a glass of milk, which Oliver accepted gratefully. The dairy helped calm the fire, but the damage was done. His eyes were red-rimmed, his nose running, and a large water stain spread across the front of his blue shirt.

'Better?' Danielle asked after a moment, her composure forced.

'Much,' Oliver croaked. 'Sorry about that.'

She offered a smile that didn't quite reach her eyes. 'We all have our weaknesses.'

The remainder of the meal passed with stilted conversation, the easy flow from earlier gone. Oliver tried to recover, asking about her hobbies and family, but there was an undeniable awkwardness that hadn't been there before. The shared glances from nearby tables didn't help.

When the bill came, Oliver insisted on paying, a small compensation for the spectacle he'd created.

Danielle didn't protest.

Outside the restaurant, the night air cool against his face, they faced each other in that peculiar end-of-date moment when intentions are decided.

'This was . . . memorable,' Danielle said with a kind smile.

'One for the record books,' Oliver agreed, attempting a light reply.

'I had a nice time, Oliver. You're a good guy.' The words were genuine but carried a finality that both knew.

'You too—I mean, you're great,' he fumbled. 'I hope Seattle works out. They'd be lucky to have you.'

She nodded, seeming relieved he'd understood. 'I hope you find someone who loves your farm as much as you do.'

Danielle reached up and kissed his cheek, and Oliver watched as she walked to her car, her heels clicking confidently on the pavement.

The drive home was quiet, just the steady hum of his truck's engine and the occasional ping of the cooling radiator. Fields of sugar cane stretched out in the darkness on either side of the road, familiar and comforting. Star-scattered sky above, open land all around. This was his world, and it felt right.

Oliver sighed, turning onto the dirt road that led to the farmhouse. Dating was exhausting. Maybe Amelia was right that he needed to find balance, but these manufactured meetings weren't the answer. He wanted something real, something that felt natural.

As he parked in the shed, he wondered if Sarah ever thought about him, too, or if he'd just been another farmer at another market stand to her.

He went inside, but the house was quiet. Looked like Amelia and Guy were both out. Oliver yawned and headed to bed. They had an early start tomorrow.

As he closed his eyes, he thought about the changes he'd noticed in Guy lately. His brother had always been the steady, reliable one—content with his spreadsheets and working on the farm—but twice this week, Oliver had caught him on the phone, speaking slow Spanish, which he'd apparently been learning from language apps. And yesterday, Elena Santiago had been in their office, bent over irrigation maps with Guy, their heads close together as they discussed water conservation techniques with an intensity that seemed to transcend professional interest.

Oliver smiled to himself. Perhaps both Johnson brothers were experiencing unexpected complications in their carefully ordered lives this summer.

Chapter 8

The mango trees stood in neat rows at the eastern edge of the farm, their leaves glossy in the morning light. Oliver moved deliberately between them, canvas bag slung across his chest, inspecting each fruit closely. The first mangoes of the season were finally ready—their skin blushing from green to a deep amber-red, yielding just slightly to the press of his thumb.

He lifted one to his nose and inhaled the sweet, tropical fragrance. Instantly, an image of Sarah formed in his mind—her pleased expression as she'd tasted a sample slice last year, the way she'd closed her eyes momentarily to savour the sweetness. He remembered how she'd held Jett up to see the colourful display, his eyes wide with curiosity.

'First harvest is looking good,' Guy called from two trees over, interrupting Oliver's thoughts.

'Yeah,' Oliver replied, carefully placing another perfectly ripe mango into his bag. 'Should have a decent selection for Friday's market.'

'Weather report's favourable too,' Guy added. 'Clear skies predicted. Bargara might give you a whole new customer base.'

Oliver nodded, feeling an unexpected flutter of anticipation that had little to do with potential sales. He'd be scanning the market looking for Sarah's stall. The logical part of his brain tried to dismiss the impulse—she might have moved away, might set up at a different market now, might not even remember him. But she had mentioned the beach markets when they'd talked last year.

His hopes lifted.

'You seem distracted,' Guy observed, moving closer with his own half-filled bag. 'Thinking about that disastrous date again?'

Oliver laughed. 'God, no. That memory is safely buried.' The water pitcher incident had quickly become family legend, much to his chagrin.

'So, what then?'

Oliver hesitated, feeling strangely vulnerable. 'Nothing really. I was just wondering if I'll see some of last year's customers over there now that the mangoes are in.'

Guy raised an eyebrow but didn't press further. They worked in companionable silence for another hour, the bags gradually filling with perfectly ripened fruit. The cane was thriving this season—the new irrigation system proving its worth, the expanded greenhouse allowing them to diversify their offerings, the small orchard finally producing at capacity.

As Oliver reached for a particularly fine specimen hanging just overhead, he allowed himself to examine his regret. 'I should have called her,' he murmured to himself, so quietly that Guy, just a few trees away, couldn't hear. 'Before I lost her phone number.'

***

'Mummy, can I mix the blue one now?' Jett asked, perched on his special step stool at the workbench.

Sarah smiled at her son's enthusiasm. 'Not yet, sweetheart. We need to wait for the red batch to set completely.' She gestured toward the rows of soap moulds cooling on the rack. 'Remember what happened last time we rushed?'

Jett's face scrunched in serious consideration. 'They got all swirly together.'

'Exactly. And while swirly can be pretty, these Christmas shop orders need to look just like the samples we showed them.'

Her small workshop, converted from what had once been a dining room, hummed with quiet productivity. Shelves lined the walls, filled with neatly labelled containers of essential oils, botanical additives, and natural colourants. A large calendar dominated one wall, dates marked in various colours denoting markets, deliveries, and production schedules.

The second Friday in December at Bargara Beach was circled in bold red—the special holiday market that could make or break her entire season. Four local Christmas shops had placed substantial pre-orders, contingent on seeing the final products at the holiday market. It was the opportunity she'd been working towards all year.

Sarah checked her watch. 'Two more hours until we need to pick up your dinosaur backpack from Miss Elaine's.' With Jett now attending daycare one full day a week, she could focus on building inventory without constant interruptions, though she treasured these mother-son production days too.

'Will we go to the farmers' market tomorrow?' Jett asked, carefully arranging dried lavender buds on a piece of wax paper.

'Yes, we need to get vegetables for the week, and maybe some of those strawberries you liked.'

Jett's eyes lit up. 'And mangoes? From the mango man?'

Sarah felt a small jolt at the nickname Jett had given Oliver after their very first meeting. 'The mangoes might not be ready yet, sweetie.'

'But you said summer is mango time. It's summer now.' His logic was impeccable.

'You're right,' Sarah conceded. 'We can certainly check.'

She turned back to her work, measuring oils with precision while her mind wandered. The dating app still sent her daily notifications, profiles of men who had "expressed interest". She'd scrolled through dozens, even exchanged messages with a few, but hadn't accepted any date invitations. Each potential match felt forced, like a jigsaw piece being jammed into the wrong space.

Elaine had gently pushed her to give someone a chance— 'You can't find connection if you don't open the door to possibility,' she'd insisted during their last coffee afternoon. Sarah knew her friend was right, but something held her back.

'Maybe the mango man will remember us,' Jett said suddenly, as if reading her thoughts.

Sarah smiled, trying to keep her expression neutral. 'Maybe he will. But remember, farmers' markets are very busy places, and he talks to lots of people.'

'But he called me "the mango expert" and let me pick the best one.' Jett said confidently.

The memory warmed her—Oliver's gentle patience with Jett's many questions, the easy way he'd included her son in their conversation. No talking over his head or exaggerated baby voice like so many adults use with children. Just genuine respect.

'We'll see,' Sarah said, not wanting to build up either of their hopes. 'But either way, we'll get some delicious fruits and vegetables.'

As she poured the melted soap base into another set of moulds, Sarah caught herself smoothing her hair, wondering if she should trim it before Friday. The realisation made her laugh at herself—primping for a chance encounter with a man who probably wouldn't even remember her name.

'What's funny, Mummy?'

'Nothing important,' she replied, helping Jett sprinkle dried roses across the tops of the cooling soap bars. 'Just grown-up silliness.'

Later, after the house had settled into evening quiet, Sarah found herself scrolling mindlessly through her phone. The dating app notification showed twelve new potential matches. She opened it out of habit, then closed it just as quickly.

Instead, she pulled up her calendar, looking at the carefully planned production schedule leading up to the December holiday market. The business was growing—slowly but steadily—and with Jett starting half-day preschool in February, she'd have more consistent work time. Things were falling into place, piece by piece.

She didn't need a relationship to complete the picture. But as she set her alarm for an early production start the next morning, she couldn't help but wonder if Oliver still had her phone number; she'd impulsively scribbled it on the back of a docket. Probably not. Who kept a random phone number?

He'd probably forgotten her.

Besides, he'd never called

Sarah turned off her bedside lamp, dreams of mangoes and market days following her into sleep.

Chapter 9

'You grow the food, but can you cook it?' Tina had asked teasingly when they matched on the app, her profile photo showing her triumphantly holding up a plate of something that looked professionally plated. The question had seemed innocent enough, even charming. A fourth date after the disaster with Danielle hadn't been in Oliver's plans, but Amelia had been relentless—'Come on, Oli. Just one last try before you throw in the towel!'

Now, standing in Tina's immaculate kitchen with its granite countertops and gleaming appliances that looked like they belonged in a cooking show, Oliver was beginning to regret his bravado.

'I'm no chef, but I know my way around basic ingredients,' he'd written back. A statement that, while not technically a lie, was proving to be a significant stretch of the truth.

'These tomatoes are gorgeous,' Tina said, examining the Marmande heirloom tomatoes he'd brought from the farm. Her auburn hair was pulled back in a practical ponytail, and she wore a patterned apron over casual clothes. 'Perfect for the sauce.'

'Thanks,' Oliver replied, relaxing slightly at the familiar topic. 'It's been a good year for them. This variety is particularly sweet.'

'So are you, Oliver.' Tina smiled, her green eyes crinkling at the corners. 'Well, let's get started then. I thought we could make pasta from scratch—nothing too complicated. I do it all the time.'

Oliver nodded with feigned confidence, rolling up his sleeves. He could handle this. After all, how different could cooking be from following the precise measurements for organic fertiliser blends?

'You can measure out the flour while I get the eggs ready,' Tina instructed, pointing to a glass jar on the counter.

Oliver meticulously measured two cups of flour as directed, creating a small mountain on the wooden cutting board. Cooking was just science, he reasoned. Precise measurements, controlled reactions.

'Now make a well in the centre for the eggs,' Tina guided, cracking three eggs into a small bowl.

Following her instructions, Oliver poured the eggs into the crater he'd formed and began mixing with a fork as she demonstrated.

'You seem to know what you're doing after all,' she observed with a smile.

'I'm a quick study,' he replied, not mentioning that this was the furthest he'd ever ventured into cuisine beyond grilling vegetables or boiling pasta from a packet.

As they worked side by side, conversation flowed easily. Tina was a high school biology teacher with a passion for sustainable living, which had prompted her interest in Oliver's profile. She asked thoughtful questions about the farm's operations, sharing her own experiences with a small backyard garden.

'The sauce needs some sugar to balance the acidity,' Tina said as they moved on to the next stage, the pasta dough resting under a towel. 'Can you add about a tablespoon to the tomatoes?'

Oliver surveyed the collection of similar-looking containers on the counter. Grabbing what he assumed was sugar, he measured a heaping tablespoon and added it to the simmering pot.

'So how long have you been teaching?' he asked, stirring the sauce.

'Almost eight years now. I started right after—' Tina paused mid-sentence, her nose wrinkling as she leaned over the pot. 'Wait, did you just add salt to the sauce?'

Oliver froze, spoon in mid-stir. 'I thought it was sugar.'

Tina grabbed the container he'd used and burst into laughter. 'Oh no, that's definitely salt. A lot of salt.'

Oliver's face flushed with embarrassment. 'I'm sorry. I should have asked first.'

She waved off his apology, still chuckling. 'Don't worry about it. We can start over with the sauce. Fortunately, I've got more tomatoes.'

Her easy forgiveness made Oliver relax again. They salvaged what vegetables they could from the over-salted disaster and began a new sauce, this time with Tina clearly pointing out which container held the sugar.

'My turn to confess,' she said as they worked. 'I kill every houseplant I own. My students find it hilarious that their biology teacher can't keep a fern alive.'

Oliver smiled, appreciating her attempt to make him feel better.

When it came time to roll out the pasta dough, they stood shoulder to shoulder at the counter, working together to create thin, even sheets. The kitchen was warm, filled with the aroma of simmering tomatoes and herbs. It felt nice, this shared creation, even with his earlier blunder.

'Now for the garlic bread,' Tina said after they'd hung the pasta strands over a wooden dowel to dry slightly. 'Can you light the oven for me?'

Oliver approached the gas stove, examining the unfamiliar knobs and buttons. Growing up with electric and then cooking on a simple gas camping stove at the farmhouse had left him unprepared for this sophisticated appliance.

'Just turn the knob and press the ignition button,' Tina called over her shoulder as she sliced a baguette.

Oliver did as instructed, turning the knob and pressing what he thought was the ignition.

Nothing happened. He tried again, turning the knob further. The faint smell of gas prompted him to keep pressing buttons.

'I don't think it's—' he began, just as he found a box of matches on the counter. 'Ah, maybe these will help.'

In retrospect, the mistake was obvious. The gas had been flowing freely as he struck the match, creating a sudden whoosh of flame that caught the kitchen towel hanging nearby.

'Fire!' Oliver yelped, instinctively grabbing for the burning towel and then dropping it when it singed his fingers.

Tina spun around, eyes widening at the flames now spreading across her counter. With remarkable composure, she grabbed a pot lid and slammed it down on the burning towel, then quickly turned off the gas.

'Are you okay?' she asked, concern evident as she checked his hand.

'Just surprised,' Oliver replied, mortified. The reddening mark on his fingers was nothing compared to the blow to his pride. 'I'm so sorry about your towel. And your counter.'

Tina surveyed the damage—a scorched dish

towel, a blackened spot on her otherwise pristine counter, and the lingering smell of burnt cotton in the air. Then, unexpectedly, she began to laugh.

'This is definitely the most memorable cooking date I've ever had,' she managed between fits of giggles. 'Maybe we should order a pizza delivery?'

Relief washed over Oliver as he joined her laughter. 'I think that's safest for both of us. And your kitchen.'

Twenty minutes later, they sat at Tina's dining table with an extra-large supreme pizza between them, glasses of wine in hand, recounting the evening's disasters with the self-deprecating humour of new friends.

'I knew I was in trouble when you called flour "the white powder stuff" while we were making the pasta dough,' Tina teased.

'I should have been honest about my cooking skills,' Oliver admitted. 'Or lack thereof.'

'Where's the fun in that?' she replied, raising her glass in a mock toast. 'To kitchen adventures!'

As the evening wound down, Oliver helped Tina clean up the remains of their cooking. The easy conversation continued, touching on things they had in common. He enjoyed her company, but when he left, the brief hug they shared confirmed what Oliver had known throughout the evening. There was friendship here, genuine and warm, but no spark—no quickening of pulse or lingering glance that suggested something more.

Tina seemed to arrive at the same conclusion. 'This was fun,' she said sincerely. 'We should do it again sometime—maybe with less fire.'

'Definitely,' Oliver agreed, knowing they probably wouldn't. 'Thanks for being so understanding about the cooking disasters.'

'That's what makes a good story,' she replied with a warm smile.

Driving home, Oliver smiled, despite the evening's mishaps. Tina had been great, kind, funny, and intelligent. On paper, a perfect match. Yet something had been missing: the chemistry. Maybe it didn't exist; maybe that was in Amelia's romance novels.

But then he thought about Charlotte and Greg, and Julien and Emily. You could see the chemistry there, just being with them.

Four dates through the app, each pleasant enough in its own way (barring the hot pepper incident), yet none had sparked anything resembling the easy connection he'd felt in those brief conversations with Sarah.

As he turned into the farm, Oliver made a decision. He was done with the app, done with the awkward first meetings and manufactured scenarios designed to create romance. If a connection happened, it would be unplanned.

Then again, maybe romance simply wasn't for him. He had the farm, his work, and friends who were practically family. It was enough. It had to be.

But as he entered the quiet house—Amelia and Guy must have gone to bed—kicking off his boots and settling into the worn leather armchair by the window, Oliver couldn't help but think of the market tomorrow. Of mangoes carefully arranged in wooden crates. Of the possibility, however slim, of a familiar face at a craft stall.

Chapter 10

In her bedroom at the farmhouse, surrounded by online craft store catalogues and hair dye swatches, Amelia scrolled idly through the CountryConnections app. She'd been spending more time on it lately, not just for Oliver's sake but for her curiosity. The dating scene in rural Queensland was a fascinating social system.

'Let's see who else is out there for Oli,' she muttered, flipping through potential matches. Her brother's reluctance to embrace modern dating was frustrating, but she remained convinced the right woman was out there, just a swipe away.

It had been nearly three weeks since Oliver's disastrous movie date with Brittany, and almost a week since his awkward dinner with Danielle. The cooking debacle with Tina had happened just two nights ago. Despite all these failures, Amelia wasn't ready to give up on her mission to find Oliver someone special.

She paused on a recently activated profile, drawn to a photo of a woman with warm eyes and an engaging smile, standing beside a craft stall at what looked like a farmers' market. Her profile mentioned handcrafted jewellery, being a single mother to a young son, and a love of local produce.

Something about the image tugged at Amelia's memory. She zoomed in on the background of the photo, noticing colourful market stalls. One corner of the frame showed crates of what appeared to be fruit.

'Wait a minute—' Excitement filled her, and her fingers flew over the keys as she quickly opened her phone's gallery, scrolling back through photos from the markets. She'd taken dozens of pictures last year, including several of the family at Oliver's mango stall.

In the background of a selfie with her friend Megan was the same craft stall from the dating profile. And standing beside it, talking animatedly with Oliver, was the woman from the dating app. She'd never noticed the background of that photo before.

'Oh my God,' Amelia whispered, her eyes widening as connections formed rapidly in her mind. 'It's her. The market girl.'

Oliver had been deflated when she'd seemingly disappeared, checking the Dunmora markets for weeks afterwards.

Amelia studied the profile more carefully. Sarah Matthews, twenty-four, jewellery designer, single mother to a four-year-old son, Bargara resident.

'So, she's been at the Bargara markets, not Dunmora,' Amelia realised, pieces falling into place. Oliver had been looking in the wrong location all this time. Her finger hovered over the "Connect" button, her mind racing with possibilities. This wasn't just another potential date—this was the woman Oliver had been pining over for nearly a year, the one he'd mentioned at family dinners, the one who'd made him smile in a way Amelia hadn't seen before or since.

But simply telling Oliver would be too straightforward, too easily dismissed. He'd find a reason not to reach out, convinced that too much time had passed or that Sarah wouldn't remember him. Or be interested in him.

'This calls for something more creative,' Amelia decided, a plan forming. She'd need a different approach—one that brought them together without either realising until it was too late to back out.

Nodding, she tapped the 'Connect' button, then navigated to Oliver's profile settings. A few quick edits would ensure Sarah wouldn't recognise him immediately—a different display name, some adjusted details. Nothing dishonest, just strategic omissions.

'Sorry, Oli,' she murmured, changing his display name to James Hayes, using their mother's maiden name. 'You can thank me later.'

Next, she composed a thoughtful message to Sarah from "James," mentioning an interest in local crafts and suggesting they might have crossed paths at farmers' markets in the region.

As she sent the message, Amelia felt a flutter of excitement. If her hunch was right, these two people who had been missing each other for months would finally get a second chance. All they needed was a little push—and possibly a reservation at the best restaurant in Bundaberg.

'Operation Market Reunion is officially underway,' she announced to her empty bedroom, already envisioning how she'd coordinate their meeting without either suspecting her involvement until the perfect moment.

***

The early morning sunlight filtered through the kitchen window, casting long shadows across the worn wooden table where Oliver sat nursing his second cup of coffee. A thin layer of soil still caked his fingernails despite his thorough scrubbing—evidence of the pre-dawn hours he'd spent with Guy checking irrigation lines. He looked up as Amelia bounced in, and he scowled.

'What are you so bubbly about? It's not even seven o'clock.'

'Just happy,' she said with a wide grin.

'Why?'

She shrugged and headed for the kettle.

'I want you to delete that app today,' he announced.

Amelia paused mid-step, her hands suspended in the air. 'What? No! You can't give up now.'

Oliver sighed, running a hand through his damp hair. 'I'm done with the digital matchmaking experiment.'

'But you've barely given it a proper chance,' Amelia protested, putting her hands on her hips. 'These things take time.'

'I've given it plenty of time. Time I could have spent on actual farm work.' Oliver stood, carrying his mug to the sink. 'The mango harvest is starting, I've got the Bargara Beach markets next week, and the new greenhouse needs finishing before the first frost.'

'That's months away. It's not even Christmas yet.' Amelia's expression shifted subtly, a flicker of something passing behind her eyes. 'I thought you usually sold at the Dunmora markets? Why the change?'

'Time to try something new,' Oliver replied with a shrug. 'Bargara has more tourists, and Guy thinks we could expand our customer base. Besides, I've searched every corner of the Dunmora markets for a year now. If Sarah's still around, she's selling her crafts somewhere else.'

'What if I told you I found someone perfect?'

Oliver groaned. 'No, no and no. You said that about the last one, and I nearly burnt down her kitchen.'

'Tina wasn't perfect. Nice, yes, but not perfect.' Amelia leaned against the counter, studying her brother. 'This one's different. I can feel it.'

'Your feelings aren't exactly scientific evidence,' Oliver muttered, though there was no real bite to his words. Despite his frustration with the dating process, he could never stay properly cross with his sister for long.

'Just one more,' Amelia pleaded, clasping her hands together dramatically. 'One final date, and if it doesn't work out, I promise I'll never ever mention dating apps or romance again. I'll even help with the greenhouse construction every weekend through autumn.'

Oliver narrowed his eyes. 'Every weekend? Including the rainy ones?'

'Every single one,' she confirmed solemnly.

He considered the offer. Extra help with the greenhouse would be invaluable, especially with the expanding crop schedule Dad had planned when they got back from France. 'Fine. One last date. But that's it, Amelia. I mean it. Last one.'

Her face split into a wide grin, a reaction that

immediately triggered Oliver's suspicion.

'Why do you look like that? What have you done?'

Amelia's smile faltered slightly. 'Well... there's something I should probably tell you.'

Oliver crossed his arms, waiting.

'I may have gone in and tweaked a few things on your profile.' She spoke quickly, the words tumbling out. 'And I might have already replied to this woman. And possibly arranged a dinner date. For next Wednesday night.'

The silence that followed was deafening.

'You did what?' Oliver finally managed; his voice was dangerously quiet.

'I was trying to help!' Amelia protested. 'Your profile was too... farmy. All soil health this, and sustainable agriculture that. I added some depth, mentioned your love of reading, how you volunteer at the community garden, your hidden talent for—'

'You pretended to be me again?' Oliver interrupted, genuine anger flaring. 'That's crossing a line, Amelia. What if I meet this woman and she expects someone completely different?'

'I didn't make anything up,' she insisted. 'Everything I added is true. I just . . . highlighted your more redeemable qualities.'

Oliver shook his head in disbelief. 'And you arranged another date without even asking me?'

'You would have said no.'

'Exactly! Because it's my life, not yours to manage!'

Amelia had the grace to look contrite, shoulders slumping slightly. 'I know. I'm sorry. I got carried away. But, Oliver, her profile—you should see it. She's smart and funny and runs her own business. She loves farmers' markets and cooking with fresh ingredients.'

'I've heard all that before.' Oliver's eyebrows shot up.

'What difference does that make?' Amelia challenged. 'Are you suddenly too good for women who like things you don't?'

'That's not fair and you know it,' Oliver replied, his tone softening slightly.

'It's just a date, not a marriage proposal,' Amelia pointed out. 'And from her messages, she seems very independent. The kind of woman who doesn't need saving but might enjoy some company.'

Oliver sighed deeply, the fight draining out of him. Part of him wanted to remain angry—Amelia had seriously overstepped the mark again—but another part recognised the genuine affection behind her meddling. She worried about him out here on the farm, working endless hours with only the occasional social interaction at markets or with the family.

'Where and when?' he asked tersely.

Amelia's face brightened. 'Next Wednesday night at eight. I've booked a table at Tides.'

'Tides?' Oliver repeated incredulously. 'That seafood place in Bundaberg? That's almost an hour's drive! And it's super expensive.'

'It's the best restaurant in the region,' Amelia defended. 'I wanted you to make a good impression.'

'With my credit card, I assume?'

'Of course not. It's my treat.' She paused, a mischievous glint returning to her eye. 'You might even have to stay the night.'

Oliver's glare could have withered cane stalks. 'Don't push it, sis. This is the last time. The mango season is starting, and I'll be too busy for this crap. Because that's what it is. It's not natural, and I'm over it.'

'Just give it a chance,' Amelia urged, more seriously. 'A proper chance. Wear something nice again, be open to possibility, and see what happens.'

Oliver nodded curtly, already turning to leave the kitchen. 'I need to check the eastern orchard. Tell Guy I'll meet him at the tool shed in twenty.'

As he strode across the yard, boots crunching on gravel, Oliver's irritation gradually subsided, replaced by a familiar resignation. One more date. One last obligation to fulfil before he could close this chapter and refocus entirely on the farm.

And the following week, he'd be selling at his first market of the season at Bargara. Regardless of how this final blind date went, he would be at his stall early, arranging golden-red fruit in wooden crates, scanning the crowd for a familiar face that had nothing to do with algorithms or dating profiles.

***

Sarah sat cross-legged on her sofa, a mug of

herbal tea balanced on the armrest, Jett's quiet snores drifting from his room. The house was peaceful in these late evening hours, the only sound the occasional ping from her laptop.

Another notification from the dating app.

She'd been about to delete her profile entirely when the message had arrived—different somehow from the others, more thoughtful, less formulaic. Something about the description of farm life, of finding beauty in simple moments, had caught her attention.

After weeks of disappointing interactions, she'd nearly written it off as another dead end. But the follow-up message had been unexpected, mentioning a reservation at Tides, a restaurant she'd always wanted to try but could never justify as a single-income household with a growing four-year-old.

'Last chance,' Sarah murmured to herself, taking a sip of cooling tea. 'One final attempt before I'm officially done with this whole experiment.'

She opened the app one more time, studying the profile picture—not particularly revealing, just a man standing in what appeared to be an orchard, his face hidden by a wide-brimmed hat. The description mentioned sustainable farming, a love of literature, and volunteer work at community gardens.

Something about it tugged at her memory, though she couldn't place exactly why. Perhaps just the mention of farming brought Oliver to mind, as so many things seemed to these days.

Sarah closed the laptop decisively. Next Wednesday night, she would go on this date. She would be open to the possibility, as Elaine was always encouraging her to be. And if nothing came of it, she could delete the app with the satisfaction of knowing she'd truly given it a fair chance.

Her phone buzzed with a text from Elaine, offering to watch Jett on Wednesday evening. Sarah smiled at her friend's uncanny timing—or perhaps not so uncanny, given Elaine's persistent encouragement of Sarah's dating efforts.

Thank you. I have a date. Last one! Pick him up at seven?

Elaine's response came immediately: Perfect! Wear that blue wrap dress. And HAVE FUN!

Sarah shook her head, amused by her friend's enthusiasm. The blue dress was perhaps a bit much for a first date, but after months of practical mum clothes and work attire spattered with soap materials, the thought of dressing up held appeal.

As she readied herself for bed, Sarah's mind drifted to the farmers' market scheduled at the beach for the following weekend. Jett had been asking all week if the mangoes would be there and if the mango man" would remember them.

'Don't get your hopes up, sweet boy,' she whispered to herself, echoing the gentle caution she'd offered her son. Advice she would do well to follow herself, for more reasons than one.

Chapter 11

Oliver adjusted his collar one last time before stepping through the glass doors of Tides. The restaurant was everything Amelia had described—elegant without being pretentious, with floor-to-ceiling windows overlooking the marina. Soft jazz played in the background as servers glided between tables with quiet efficiency.

'Reservation for John—I mean, Hayes,' he quickly corrected as he spoke to the hostess, glancing around at the other diners, wondering which stranger would be his final dating app attempt.

'Yes, sir. Your guest has already arrived. Right this way.'

Oliver followed, mentally rehearsing his introduction. Best to be straightforward about Amelia's interference, he decided. Start with honesty and—

He stopped abruptly, nearly colliding with the hostess when she paused at a corner table. The woman seated there looked up from her menu, and the recognition was instantaneous.

'Sarah?' The name escaped his lips before he could process what was happening.

Her eyes widened, lips parting in surprise. 'Oliver? Oliver Johnson?'

The hostess, misreading their stunned expressions for pleasant surprise, smiled. 'Enjoy your evening,' she said before discreetly retreating.

For a long moment, neither spoke. Oliver stood frozen beside the table, unable to reconcile the Sarah from the Dunmora farmers' market with the woman before him in a blue wrap dress, her hair falling in loose waves around her shoulders.

'I don't understand,' Sarah finally managed, her voice barely above a whisper. 'You're . . . James Hayes? From the app?'

'No.' He shook his head, finally regaining enough composure to slide into the chair opposite her. 'I'm Oliver Johnson from the farm. And you're Sarah. From the Dunmora markets last year.'

'Yes,' she confirmed, still looking dazed. 'This is—'

'Unexpected,' Oliver finished. What was

Amelia up to? A different name? Or was another date about to turn up here? One for him, and a James for her. Suddenly, he felt possessive.

Their eyes met, and something about the sheer improbability of the situation struck them both at once. A laugh bubbled up from Sarah's throat, tentative at first, then growing. Oliver couldn't help but join in, the tension that had been building in his shoulders for the past twenty-four hours dissolving into genuine amusement.

'I've been selling at the Bargara Beach markets for months now,' Sarah explained once their laughter subsided. 'I switched after... well, after I thought you weren't interested.'

'I looked for you at Dunmora for weeks,' Oliver admitted. 'I never thought to check Bargara.'

'I'm guessing you didn't know either?' Sarah asked, drawing curious glances from nearby tables.

'Not a clue,' Oliver confirmed, shaking his head. 'My sister Amelia set this up. She . . . well, she apparently hijacked my profile and arranged this date without telling me who you were and changing my name so you wouldn't know who I was.'

'That explains it,' Sarah said, her initial shock giving way to curiosity. 'The messages seemed a bit different in style from your profile.'

'Which I also didn't write,' Oliver admitted, running a hand through his hair. 'Amelia thought my original was too "farmy," whatever that means.'

Sarah smiled, the familiar warmth in her expression bringing Oliver back to their conversations over mangoes and soap. 'And here I was, convinced I was meeting a complete stranger for my last attempt at online dating. But you know what? I love your sister already.'

The waiter approached with water and wine menus, giving them a moment to collect their thoughts. After placing their drink orders, an awkward silence settled between them—filled with unasked questions.

'So,' they both began simultaneously, then laughed again, some of the awkwardness dissipating.

'Ladies first,' Oliver offered.

Sarah took a deep breath. 'I've been

wondering . . . why didn't you ever call me?' The question had been circling in her mind for a year, and seeing him sitting across from her now, it simply tumbled out.

Oliver's expression turned rueful. 'I meant to. I really did.' He hesitated before continuing. 'I kept your number in my wallet for days, taking it out almost every night, telling myself I'd call the next day when I wasn't so tired from harvest.'

He met her eyes directly, honesty evident in his gaze. 'Then one day I went to pay for something and realised it wasn't there anymore. I tore apart my truck, my house, everywhere I could think of. Never found it. By then, so much time had passed, I figured you'd think I was strange for suddenly calling out of the blue if I did find it.'

'I would have been happy to hear from you,' Sarah said quietly, surprised by her own candour. 'Even out of the blue.'

The waiter returned with their drinks, taking their dinner orders before leaving them to their conversation once more.

'Can I ask you something?' Oliver ventured once they were alone again.

Sarah nodded.

'Your son—Jett, right? I've been remembering bits and pieces from our market conversations. How is he?'

Sarah's expression softened at the mention of Jett, but Oliver noticed a hint of wariness too. 'He's wonderful. Growing too fast, talking constantly, obsessed with anything that grows.' She paused, studying Oliver's face. 'You remember him?'

'Of course,' Oliver replied, genuinely surprised by the question. 'The mango expert. Small guy, big questions.' He smiled at the memory. 'He's hard to forget.'

'Most men I've met seem to view single motherhood as a drawback,' Sarah admitted. 'Something to be tolerated rather than embraced.'

'Those men are idiots,' Oliver stated flatly, then looked slightly abashed at his own bluntness. 'I mean—children are part of who you are. That's not a negative.'

Sarah felt something tight in her chest begin to loosen. 'You knew he was my son? I wondered if you might have thought he was my little brother or something.'

Oliver looked genuinely surprised. 'No, it was pretty clear he was yours from the way you interacted.'

A comfortable silence settled between them before Sarah spoke again, her voice quieter. 'His father died before Jett was born. A motorcycle accident.' She rarely shared this detail so early, but something about Oliver's straightforward acceptance of Jett made her want to be equally open. 'We weren't together when it happened— it was a summer thing that had ended a few weeks before. I didn't even know I was pregnant then.'

Oliver's expression held simple compassion without the awkward pity she often encountered. 'That must have been incredibly difficult.'

'It was,' Sarah acknowledged. 'But also strangely . . . clarifying. Nothing focuses your priorities like becoming a single parent unexpectedly.'

'Is that when you started your business?' Oliver asked.

Sarah nodded, grateful for his perceptiveness. 'I needed something flexible, something I could build while being home with Jett. Something that was mine.'

'You've done an amazing job,' Oliver said, his admiration evident. 'With both your business and Jett.'

'Thank you,' Sarah replied, feeling unexpectedly emotional at the simple acknowledgment. 'Ryan—Jett's father—he was adventurous, always seeking the next thrill. I see that in Jett sometimes, that fearlessness.'

'And the curiosity,' Oliver added with a smile. 'The way he examines everything so carefully before making up his mind.'

'That he gets from me,' Sarah laughed softly. 'Poor kid got my overthinking tendencies.'

'I wouldn't call it overthinking,' Oliver corrected gently. 'More like... thoroughness. It's a good quality.'

As their conversation shifted to other topics, Sarah felt a quiet sense of relief. Sharing Jett's origin story often created awkwardness, but Oliver had received it as simply another part of who they were—not a complication or a burden, but their history, honoured with the respect it deserved.

As they shared dessert—a mango sorbet that both agreed wasn't as good as fresh mangoes from Oliver's farm—Sarah realised how different this felt from her other dating attempts. There was no forced conversation, no mental calculation of compatibility factors. Just the easy rapport they'd discovered a year ago, now given room to breathe and expand.

When the bill arrived, they both reached for it simultaneously.

'Please, let me,' Oliver insisted. 'Technically, my sister invited you, so it's only fair.'

'Next time, then,' Sarah replied, then realised the implication of her words. 'I mean— if there is a—'

'I'd like that,' Oliver said simply, saving her from her stammering. 'Very much.'

Outside, the night air was cool and clear, stars visible despite the marina lights. Oliver walked beside Sarah toward the parking lot, close enough that their hands occasionally brushed, sending small currents of awareness between them.

'Where are you parked?' he asked as they reached the first row of cars.

'Just over there,' Sarah pointed to a modest sedan a few spaces away. 'You?'

'Back corner,' Oliver nodded toward the far end of the lot. 'I'll walk you to your car.'

They moved slowly, neither seemingly eager for the evening to end. When they reached Sarah's car, she turned to face him, illuminated by the soft glow of a nearby lamppost.

'This was unexpected,' she said softly. 'But I'm glad it happened.'

'Remind me to thank Amelia,' Oliver replied, his voice equally soft. 'Though I'll never hear the end of it.'

Sarah laughed quietly, her eyes meeting his. The moment stretched between them, full of unspoken possibilities.

Oliver moved first, one hand gently cupping her cheek as he leaned down. Sarah rose slightly on her toes to meet him halfway, their lips coming together in a kiss that was gentle at first, then deepening as her arms wound around his neck.

When they finally broke apart, both slightly

breathless, Oliver rested his forehead against hers for a moment.

'I'll see you at the market Saturday next week?' he asked.

'We'll be there,' Sarah confirmed. 'Jett's been talking about mangoes all week.'

'I'll save the best ones for him,' Oliver promised, reluctantly stepping back as Sarah unlocked her car door.

'Goodnight, Oliver.'

'Goodnight, Sarah.'

He watched her drive away, remaining in the parking lot long after her taillights had disappeared. The night felt full of possibility in a way he hadn't experienced in years—perhaps ever.

The drive home passed in a blur, his mind replaying moments from the evening: Sarah's laugh, the way she listened so intently when he spoke of the farm, the softness of her lips against his. For once, the farm wasn't the last thing he thought about before falling asleep.

The market day couldn't come soon enough, but with over a week to wait, Oliver knew he'd need to find the patience that farming had taught him. Good things, like the perfect mangoes, couldn't be rushed.

Chapter 12

Oliver arrived at the farmers' market before dawn, the eastern sky just beginning to lighten from black to deep purple. The familiar routine of setting up his stall—unfolding tables, arranging crates, positioning the hand-painted "Johnson Family Farm" sign—normally centred him, but today his movements were rushed and distracted.

He'd selected the mangoes with extra care, culling through the morning's harvest for the most perfect specimens—unblemished, fragrant, with that perfect give when gently pressed. The premium fruit always went to market, but today he'd brought truly exceptional pieces, arranging them in wooden crates lined with green tissue paper that made the golden-red skin glow.

'Someone's in a good mood,' Guy remarked, helping unload the last of the produce from the truck. 'You're whistling.'

'Am I?' Oliver hadn't noticed.

'Yep. Same tune for the past twenty minutes.' Guy studied his friend's face. 'I take it the date wasn't as disastrous as predicted?'

Oliver arranged a display of heirloom tomatoes, trying and failing to suppress a smile. 'It was . . . unexpected.'

'Unexpected good or unexpected bad?'

'Good. Definitely good,' Oliver admitted. 'Turns out I already knew her.'

Guy's eyebrows shot up. 'No kidding? Who—' He stopped mid-question as realisation dawned. 'Wait. Not the market woman? The one with the kid who loves mangoes?'

Oliver nodded, pleased he wouldn't have to explain the whole story.

'Well, I'll be damned,' Guy laughed, clapping Oliver on the shoulder. 'Amelia will be insufferable when she finds out her meddling actually worked.'

'She doesn't know yet,' Oliver said. 'And I'd appreciate keeping it that way until after market hours. I need time to process everything without her twenty questions.'

'Your secret's safe with me,' Guy promised. 'But I want details later.'

As Guy headed back to the truck for another crate, Oliver's attention was caught by movement at the empty stall space beside his.

The market organisers had been setting up a stall next to his, something about adjusting the layout for better customer flow. He hadn't paid much attention when they'd assigned him his spot earlier.

Now, a familiar figure was unfolding a portable table. Oliver froze, his hands still holding a mango mid-arrangement.

Sarah.

She hadn't noticed him yet, her back turned as she carefully laid out a folding display rack. Her hair was pulled back in a practical ponytail, and she wore a simple sundress with a denim jacket against the early morning chill.

'Need a hand with that?' Oliver found himself saying before his brain had fully caught up.

Sarah turned, the display rack wobbling precariously in her hands. Her eyes widened in surprise, then lit up with recognition and pleasure.

'Oliver?' The rack tilted dangerously, and he stepped forward quickly to steady it. 'What are you—' Her gaze shifted to his stall, understanding dawning. 'You're my neighbour!'

'Looks that way,' he replied, unable to keep the smile from his face. 'The market gods have a sense of humour.'

'Or the universe is trying to tell us something,' Sarah said with a small laugh. The warmth in her eyes made his heart do that strange flip it seemed to manage only in her presence.

'Where's Jett?' Oliver asked, helping her set the display rack down securely.

'With Elaine at the jam stall. She's giving him breakfast—I had to set up early, and he was still half-asleep.' Sarah glanced at Oliver's meticulously arranged mangoes. 'Those look amazing.'

'More picking yesterday,' he said, following her gaze. 'Picked the best ones for today.'

A significant look passed between them, acknowledgment of their unexpected dinner date hanging in the air.

'Mummy!' A small voice called out excitedly. They turned to see Jett running toward them, dodging between early market-goers with Elaine following at a more sedate pace. The boy skidded to a stop, his eyes growing wide as he registered Oliver standing beside his mother.

'The mango man!' he exclaimed, his whole face lighting up. 'Mummy, the mango man is right next to us!'

'I see that,' Sarah replied, smiling at her son's enthusiasm. 'What a nice surprise.'

'Hello, mango expert,' Oliver said, crouching down to meet Jett at eye level. 'Want to see this year's crop?'

Jett nodded vigorously, practically vibrating with excitement.

'Perfect timing,' Elaine said as she reached them, her knowing eyes darting between Sarah and Oliver. 'I was just bringing this little man back to help set up, but I see you've found some . . . assistance.' The emphasis she placed on the word made Sarah's cheeks colour slightly.

'Elaine, this is Oliver Johnson,' Sarah introduced. 'Oliver, this is Elaine, my market mentor and Jett's honorary grandmother.'

'The famous mango farmer,' Elaine said, giving Oliver an appraising once-over that made him feel like he was being evaluated for far more than his fruit-growing abilities. 'Sarah's mentioned you.'

'Has she?' Oliver couldn't help glancing at

Sarah, who was suddenly very interested in arranging her soap display.

'Mummy said your mangoes are the best in Queensland,' Jett supplied helpfully, earning a stifled laugh from Elaine and an even deeper blush from Sarah.

'Did she now?' Oliver felt an absurd burst of pride.

'I may have said something along those lines,' Sarah admitted.

'Well, I'll leave you young people to your setup,' Elaine announced. 'My jams won't arrange themselves. Sarah, dear, we'll catch up later.' The significant look she gave Sarah spoke volumes.

As the market officially opened at seven, the usual early birds began trickling in. Having neighbouring stalls created a unique dynamic—Oliver and Sarah could chat between customers, share observations, and watch each other's spaces during brief breaks. Jett alternated between helping his mother arrange her soaps and sitting at a small folding table beside Oliver's stall, drawing pictures and occasionally assisting as Oliver's "official mango selection consultant".

By nine o'clock, the market was in full swing. During a rare quiet moment, Oliver leaned against the side of his stall, watching as Sarah wrapped a purchase for a customer.

'This is nice,' he said when the customer had left. 'Being neighbours.'

'It is,' she agreed, adjusting her display. 'Though a bit distracting.'

'Am I distracting you?' Oliver asked with a grin.

'You know you are,' Sarah replied, a smile playing at the corners of her mouth. 'I've nearly given the wrong change twice.'

'I'll try to be less . . . whatever it is,' he promised, not sounding particularly sincere.

Sarah laughed. 'Please don't.'

During a lull in customers, both of them watched as Jett concentrated on his drawing, tongue poking out slightly in focus.

'I really did lose your number,' Oliver said suddenly, picking up their conversation from their dinner date. 'I must have pulled out a note and not noticed it came out with too. But—'

'But what?' Sarah prompted gently when he

didn't continue.

Oliver met her eyes. 'I wasn't sure if you'd want me to call anyway. We'd only met that time. I thought maybe I'd imagined something that wasn't really there.'

Sarah nodded, understanding. 'I wondered if you'd found out I was a single mum and decided it wasn't worth the complication.' She glanced at Jett, lowering her voice. 'It's happened before. Men seem interested until they realise Jett is part of the package.'

'That wasn't it at all,' Oliver assured her. 'Honestly, I thought you were probably just being nice to the guy who sold you mangoes.'

Sarah laughed softly. 'I'm nice to lots of people who sell me things. I don't give them all my number.'

The admission hung between them, simple but significant.

'Look, Mummy! I drew the farm!' Jett interrupted, holding up his drawing proudly. What appeared to be trees, a house, and several stick figures covered the page in vibrant crayon colours.

'It's beautiful, sweetie,' Sarah praised,

accepting the artwork. 'Who are all these people?'

'That's me,' Jett pointed to a small figure. 'And that's you. And that's the mango man.'

Oliver peered at the drawing, touched by his inclusion in the boy's imagination. 'You've even got the orchard rows right. Very accurate.'

Jett beamed at the praise. 'Can I see the real farm sometime?'

The question caught both adults off guard. Sarah looked momentarily flustered, unsure how to respond to her son's directness.

'I think that would be great,' Oliver said carefully, holding Sarah's gaze. 'If your mummy thinks it's a good idea.'

'We'll see,' Sarah told Jett, stroking his hair. 'The farm is very busy, especially during harvest.'

'Actually,' Oliver said, an idea forming, 'we're having a small harvest festival next month. Nothing fancy, just some families from Duckinwilla Creek coming to pick their own fruit, hayrides for the kids, that sort of thing. You both would be welcome.'

Sarah considered this, clearly appreciating

the casual nature of the invitation. 'That sounds nice. We'll have to check our calendar.'

Oliver nodded, understanding her caution. Their connection was wonderful but still new. In the light of day, with Jett present, the reality of their situation required more careful navigation. Sarah wasn't just thinking about her own heart but her son's as well.

The day passed quickly, with both of them steadily selling their wares. When Jett grew restless in the afternoon, Oliver showed him how to arrange the mangoes by colour gradient, a task the little boy took to with serious dedication. Sarah watched them together, her expression soft.

As the market began to wind down, Sarah looked over at Oliver. 'This has been one of my best market days in months.'

'The soap business booming?' Oliver asked.

'That too,' she said with a smile. 'But I meant having you next to us. It's been nice.'

'I'll have to thank the market organiser for the placement,' Oliver said. 'Though I'm not sure my total focus was on selling mangoes today.'

'Mine wasn't entirely on soap either,' Sarah admitted.

As they began packing up their respective stalls, Oliver selected a small crate of his finest mangoes. 'For the mango expert and his mum,' he said, placing it on Sarah's folded table.

'We can't take all those,' Sarah protested.

'Course you can,' Oliver insisted. 'They're perfect right now—be a shame to let them sit.'

'Will I see you again soon?' Oliver asked, not quite ready for them to leave.

Sarah smiled, the warmth reaching her eyes. 'We come to the market most Saturdays. And there's that harvest festival to consider.'

'I could call you,' Oliver suggested. 'If I had your number. Again.'

'You could,' Sarah agreed, reaching into her bag for a business card. This time, she wrote her number directly on the front. 'And maybe take care when you open your wallet.'

Oliver laughed, tucking the card carefully into his shirt pocket, patting it twice for good measure. 'I've learned my lesson.'

As they said their goodbyes, Jett surprised Oliver with a quick hug around his legs before darting back to his mother's side. The simple gesture affected Oliver more deeply than he could have anticipated.

He watched them weave through the market toward the parking area, Jett turning back once to wave enthusiastically. Something significant had shifted in his life today. The caution was still there—both of them careful not to rush forward too quickly—but beneath it lay a foundation of understanding that felt solid. Real.

For the first time, Oliver found himself thinking beyond the next harvest, the next season. Thinking of a sweet woman and her child.

And it didn't feel frightening at all.

##

The following Tuesday afternoon, Oliver invited Sarah and Jett to the farm. While Sarah helped Amelia organise kitchen supplies for the upcoming harvest festival, Oliver took Jett out to the chicken coop. The warm Queensland sun filtered through the gum trees, casting dappled shadows across the gravel path as they made their way toward the weathered structure.

'Do you know how to check for eggs?'

Oliver asked, holding the wooden gate open for the boy.

'I do.' Jett nodded solemnly, his four-year-old face serious with concentration. 'You have to be gentle. And you look under the hens very carefully.'

Oliver smiled, handing Jett the small collection basket he'd found in the shed. 'That's right. And you have to stay away from Mr. Cranky Pants.'

'Mr Cranky Pants,' Jett giggled, eyeing the large red rooster who watched them suspiciously from his perch. 'He doesn't like visitors.'

'Good memory,' Oliver praised as they stepped into the coop, the familiar scent of hay and feed greeting them. The hens clucked softly, already accustomed to Jett's careful approach after his few visits.

'Did you know my real dad?' Jett asked suddenly as they collected eggs together, the question catching Oliver off guard with its directness.

Oliver carefully placed another egg in the basket before answering. 'No, I didn't have the chance to meet him.'

Jett nodded, accepting this. 'He died before I was borned. On a motorbike.'

'Your mum told me,' Oliver said gently. 'I'm sorry that happened.'

Jett seemed to be working through something, his small face scrunched in concentration. 'Mom says he would have loved me a whole lot.'

'I'm sure that's absolutely true,' Oliver affirmed.

'But he's not here,' Jett continued matter-of-factly. 'So he can't take me fishing or build forts or teach me to ride a bike.'

Oliver wasn't sure where this conversation was heading, but he knelt down to Jett's level, giving the boy his full attention. 'No, he can't do those things. That's really tough.'

Jett locked eyes with Oliver. 'Mummy says you have a boat. A small one for the creek.'

'I do,' Oliver confirmed. 'For fishing sometimes.'

'Could I go with you to the creek? Sometime?' Jett asked. The hope in his little face tugged at Oliver's emotions. 'Just to try it? I've never been fishing.'

'I think that sounds like a plan. If Mum says yes.'

'She will,' Jett said with surprising confidence. 'She says you're good at explaining things. Like the mangoes.' He paused, then added with devastating simplicity: 'I think my real dad would be okay with you teaching me stuff. Since he can't.'

Oliver swallowed against the unexpected tightness in his throat. 'That's a very kind thought, Jett. Thank you.'

Jett nodded, seemingly satisfied with the exchange, and returned to the serious business of egg collection.

Later, when Oliver mentioned the conversation to Sarah, her eyes filled with tears.

'He's never said anything like that before,' she whispered. 'About another man teaching him things his father would have.'

'Kids surprise you,' Oliver said. 'Just when you think you understand them.'

Sarah smiled through her tears. 'Ryan would have liked you, I think. You're different to him, but you have that knack for finding joy in simple things.'

It was the best compliment she could have given him—not that he could replace Jett's father, but what he and Sarah shared.

Chapter 13

The Johnson farmhouse, which had known a month of relative quiet, erupted into chaos once more as the minivan pulled into the driveway, kicking up dust in the late afternoon sun. Oliver, Guy, and Amelia stood on the porch, watching as doors flew open and their travel-weary family spilled out amidst exclamations, stretching limbs, and an explosion of luggage.

'Home at last!' Ellen called, her face lighting up despite obvious exhaustion. 'The French countryside was magnificent, but nothing beats the sight of home.'

Grandmère emerged next, somehow looking as put-together as if she'd just stepped out for afternoon tea rather than endured a twenty-four-hour journey. 'Oh, *mes chéris!* The farm is still standing! Guy, Oliver—you haven't burned anything down!'

'Disappointed, Grandmère?' Oliver teased, stepping forward to help with bags.

'Never, *mon petit.* Though perhaps a small kitchen fire would have been dramatic.' She patted his cheek affectionately before turning to embrace Amelia. 'Your hair! It is now blue and silver! Like the night sky!'

Amelia preened, touching her freshly dyed locks. 'Changed it last week. Thought you'd appreciate something new to come home to.'

Hugo Johnson descended from the driver's seat, looking simultaneously relieved and invigorated. 'The irrigation system held up?' he asked Guy, bypassing any conventional greeting.

'Not a single issue,' Guy confirmed with the hint of a smile. 'The new setup in the eastern field is performing thirty percent better than projected.'

'And the mangoes?' Hugo turned to Oliver.

'Harvest went perfectly. We've been selling out at the markets every weekend.'

Hugo nodded, satisfied. 'Good. Good.' Then, in an uncharacteristic move, he pulled both sons into a brief, firm hug. 'Missed you boys.'

Charlotte and Greg were the last to emerge, laden with carry-on bags and souvenirs. 'We need reinforcements!' Charlotte called. 'Papa fell asleep in the back seat, and he's sound asleep and snoring.'

'Let him rest,' Ellen advised. 'He hardly

slept on the plane. We'll get home to their place when we unload our luggage.'

As they unpacked the van, the house filled with voices calling out questions, observations, and demands.

'Where's the gift we got for Lisette? The little painting?' 'Did anyone feed my sourdough starter while we were gone?' 'Is there any food in this house? I'm starving!' 'Someone put the kettle on!' 'My legs feel like they've been folded in half for days.'

After the initial flurry subsided and Greg had left to drive Grandmère and Papa to their place, the family gathered in the kitchen where Amelia had prepared dinner. A roast chicken with vegetables sat at the centre of the table, alongside fresh bread from the bakery in town and one of Oliver's prized mangoes, cut into perfect slices.

'You three have managed well,' Ellen observed, helping herself to a glass of wine that Hugo had poured. 'The house isn't even a disaster.'

'Oli's developed some domestic skills,' Amelia said with a mischievous gleam in her eye. 'He's been cooking. And cleaning. Almost like he was trying to impress someone.'

Oliver shot her a warning glance that went completely ignored.

'Impress someone?' Charlotte perked up, her travel fatigue momentarily forgotten. 'Who?'

'No one,' Oliver replied too quickly. 'I just got tired of living in Amelia's mess.'

'My mess?' Amelia laughed. 'That's rich coming from Mr. Leaves-Mud-Covered-Boots-in-the-Hallway.'

'Actually,' Guy interjected, his quiet voice somehow cutting through the banter, 'he has been on his best behaviour lately. Even ironed a shirt last week.'

The kitchen fell silent as all eyes turned to Oliver.

'You ironed?' Ellen whispered, as if witnessing a miracle. 'A girlfriend!'

'It's not—' Oliver began, but Amelia interrupted.

'Her name is Sarah,' she announced triumphantly. 'The market girl from last year. She's back in his life, and he's been disgustingly happy about it.'

A collective gasp rippled through the room,

followed immediately by a barrage of questions.

'The one with the laugh?' Charlotte asked.

'The one with the jewellery?' Lisette's voice chimed in from the tablet that had been propped up on the counter to include her in the homecoming.

'How did this happen?' Hugo demanded, looking bewildered.

Oliver sighed, knowing resistance was futile. 'It's a long story.'

'We have time,' Ellen insisted, settling more comfortably into her chair.

Reluctantly, Oliver recounted the tale—how Amelia had hijacked his dating profile, arranged a dinner with an unknown woman who turned out to be Sarah, and how they'd reconnected after nearly a year apart.

'So, you've been seeing each other?' Charlotte pressed when he finished. 'How many dates?'

'We've been spending time together,' Oliver said carefully. 'Markets on Saturdays. She brought Jett to the farm for a visit, too.'

'Jett?' Hugo questioned.

'Her son,' Oliver explained. 'He's four.

Smart kid. Loves mangoes.'

'Well, that speaks to his good taste,' Guy murmured.

'And you like him? The boy?' Ellen asked, her expression softening.

Oliver nodded. 'He's great. Full of questions. Wants to know how everything works.'

'Just like you at that age,' Hugo observed quietly, his expression thoughtful.

'When do we get to meet them?' Ellen leaned forward eagerly.

Oliver hesitated. 'I hadn't really thought about—'

'Nonsense,' Ellen interrupted. 'Of course they must come to dinner. How about this weekend?'

'Mum, they're not—we're not—' Oliver fumbled for words. 'It's still new. I don't want to overwhelm them.'

'We won't overwhelm them,' Amelia said with a grin.

'Together, we are exhausting,' Oliver corrected, shaking his head 'And numerous. And loud. And Grandmère would want to be here too when she hears.' He frowned at Amelia. 'As I am sure she will soon, if not already?'

Amelia grinned back at him. 'Probably.'

'All the more reason for a proper introduction,' Charlotte argued. 'Better to know what she's getting into sooner rather than later.'

Oliver looked to Guy for support, but his brother merely shrugged. 'They have a point. Might as well rip off the Band-Aid.'

'Friday,' Ellen decided, already planning. 'I'll make my special roast. Charlotte, you make that lovely dessert—the one with the berries. Grandmère can share her stories about the lavender fields? She makes soap, you said? She'd appreciate that.'

Oliver watched helplessly as his family organised what was beginning to sound like an elaborate welcome ceremony rather than a simple dinner.

'I'll need to ask her first,' he reminded them. 'She might already have plans.'

Hugo smiled. 'A chance to meet the Johnson family? Who would refuse?'

***

'Your entire family?' Sarah's voice held a

note of panic even through the phone connection. 'All at once?'

Oliver paced the length of the porch, phone pressed to his ear as the sunset painted long shadows across the yard. 'I tried to postpone, but they're . . . insistent.'

'That's a diplomatic way of putting it,' Sarah replied with a nervous laugh. 'I'm not sure, Oliver. It seems like a big step.'

'It is,' he agreed. 'And if you're not comfortable with it, I'll tell them you're busy. I'm good at disappointing my family. Years of practice.'

That earned a genuine laugh. 'I'm sure that's not true.' She paused. 'Would Jett be welcome? I don't always have a sitter available.'

'Of course,' Oliver said quickly. 'They specifically included him in the invitation. My sister Amelia is already planning activities to keep him entertained.'

Another pause. 'What should I bring?'

Oliver felt a surge of hope. 'Just yourselves. Mum insists on handling everything else.'

'I can't show up empty-handed to meet your family for the first time,' Sarah protested.

'You won't be empty-handed. You'll be wrangling a four-year-old.'

'Fair point,' she conceded. 'What time?'

They worked out the details, and when Oliver hung up, he found Amelia leaning against the doorframe, arms crossed and a smug expression on her face.

'She said yes?' his sister asked, though it wasn't really a question.

'She said yes,' Oliver confirmed. 'But if anyone mentions wedding bells or French countryside honeymoons, I'm disowning the lot of you.'

Amelia mimed zipping her lips. 'We'll be on our absolute best behaviour.'

'Somehow, that's even more terrifying.'

##

Friday evening arrived with perfect early summer weather, the kind that made the farm look like a scene from a postcard—golden light spilling across green cane fields, the mango trees casting long shadows, the farmhouse glowing with welcome.

Oliver had spent the afternoon in a flurry of last-minute tidying up that earned knowing smirks from Guy and outright teasing from Amelia. By six o'clock, he'd changed his shirt twice and was contemplating a third when the sound of tyres on gravel announced Sarah's arrival.

He stepped onto the porch just as her car pulled up beside his truck. Jett was out first, bursting from the vehicle with the boundless energy of childhood.

'Are there cows too? I saw the chickens last time,' he called up to Oliver, who was descending the steps. 'Mom said there might be cows.'

'No cows, I'm afraid,' Oliver replied, unable to suppress a smile at Jett's enthusiasm. 'But we have some new kittens in the shed.'

Sarah emerged more slowly, smoothing down a simple floral dress. She looked beautiful but unmistakably nervous.

'I brought this,' she said, holding up a small basket. 'Some of my lavender soap and honey-oatmeal bath bombs. I know you said not to bring anything, but—'

'It's perfect,' Oliver assured her, briefly squeezing her hand. 'Mum and Grandmère will love it. Ready?'

Before Sarah could answer, the screen door banged open, and Ellen Johnson appeared, wiping her hands on her apron.

'You must be Sarah!' she exclaimed warmly. 'And this handsome young man must be Jett! We've heard so much about you both.'

Oliver couldn't get over the change in Mum since they'd been overseas. She glowed with happiness.

'You have?' Sarah glanced questioningly at Oliver.

'Apparently, I talk about you,' he admitted quietly. 'A lot.'

What followed was a whirlwind of introductions as the Johnson family materialised seemingly from all corners of the house. Charlotte and Greg arrived moments later with the promised berry dessert. Grandmère swept in from the living room, immediately taking Sarah's face between her hands and declaring her '*magnifique*' before launching into rapid-fire questions about soap-making techniques.

'Is it true you use real lavender? From the garden? In France, my cousin Mathilde grows the most beautiful lavender fields. The scent! *Incroyable*!'

Amelia knelt down to Jett's level, introducing herself as "the sister with the cool hair", which earned her an instant fan.

'It's blue!' Jett observed, wide-eyed.

'And silver,' Amelia confirmed. 'Like a superhero, right?'

Jett nodded solemnly. 'Or a robot princess.'

'I like the way you think, kid,' Amelia laughed. 'Want to see the kittens while the grown-ups talk about boring stuff?'

After a confirming nod from Sarah, Jett eagerly took Amelia's offered hand and disappeared toward the back door.

'He'll be completely safe with her,' Oliver assured Sarah, noting her momentary hesitation. 'Amelia's surprisingly good with kids. She just never grew up herself.'

'I heard that!' Amelia called over her shoulder.

Guy stepped forward with a friendly nod, while Hugo Johnson remained standing slightly apart, his expression difficult to read. Oliver had expected his father's immediate enthusiasm—

Hugo normally loved meeting new people connected to the farm—but tonight he seemed unusually reserved, his gaze lingering thoughtfully on Jett, who was now excitedly telling Amelia about a dinosaur he'd brought along.

Dinner itself was a boisterous affair, Ellen's roast declared a triumph, the table conversation flowing from French adventures to farm updates. Sarah answered questions about her soap business with growing confidence, but Oliver noticed his father's unusual quietness. He contributed occasionally but seemed to be observing more than participating. He began to worry that his heart was playing up again.

When Sarah excused herself to help Jett with a second serving, Hugo leaned toward Oliver.

'She seems lovely,' he said in a low voice, 'but have you really thought this through, son?'

Surprise jolted through Oliver. 'What do you mean?'

Hugo glanced toward Jett, then back to Oliver. 'Taking on a readymade family is different from starting fresh. The boy's young, impressionable. If things don't work out between you and Sarah—'

'Dad,' Oliver interrupted, keeping his voice even, 'I care about both of them. A lot.'

'I don't doubt that,' Hugo replied. 'But farming life isn't easy on relationships, even without the added complexity of a child.' He paused. 'I just want you to be sure. For everyone's sake.'

Before Oliver could respond, Sarah returned with Jett, and the conversation shifted to lighter topics. But Oliver remained aware of his father's subtle scrutiny throughout the meal, the careful way he observed Sarah and Jett's interactions.

After dessert, while Charlotte and Amelia cleared the table and Grandmère regaled Jett with tales of all the different types of cats they saw in France, Oliver found his father on the back porch, gazing out at the moonlit orchard.

'You don't approve,' Oliver said, joining him at the railing.

Hugo turned, surprised. 'That's not it.'

'Then what is it, Dad? You've barely said two words to Sarah all night. I'm sure she's noticed.'

Hugo sighed, running a hand through his

thinning hair. 'When your mother and I started out, it was just the two of us against the world. Hard enough figuring things out together without adding—' he gestured vaguely.

'A child,' Oliver finished. 'You can say it.'

'It's not that I don't like them,' Hugo clarified. 'But farming is an all-in proposition, Oliver. The hours, the stress, the uncertainty—it's why so many farming marriages fail. Add a young boy who's already lost one father figure—'

Oliver understood then. His father wasn't being judgemental—he was worried. For all of them.

'Did you know,' Oliver said carefully, 'that Jett asked me yesterday if we could plant a special mango tree just for him? So, he could watch it grow every time he visits?'

Hugo's eyebrows raised. 'Did he now?'

'He's already thinking long-term, Dad. He sees a future here.' Oliver paused. 'And so do I.'

Hugo studied his son's face, then nodded slowly. 'You know your own mind. Always have.'

Inside, they could hear Jett's delighted

laughter mixing with Grandmère's theatrical storytelling. Hugo's expression softened at the sound.

'He's a good boy,' he admitted. 'Reminds me a bit of you at that age. Full of questions.'

'He is,' Oliver agreed. 'And Sarah's done that all on her own. Imagine what she could do with a partner.'

Hugo gave his son a sidelong glance. 'Is that what you want to be? Her partner?'

'I'm figuring that out,' Oliver replied honestly. 'But I know I want the chance to try.'

Hugo clasped Oliver's shoulder, his grip firm. 'Then you have my support. Whatever you need.'

When they returned inside, Hugo approached Sarah, who was helping Jett build something with napkins and dessert spoons.

'Sarah,' he said, his voice warmer than it had been all evening, 'Oliver tells me you're interested in growing your own herbs. I've been experimenting in the kitchen garden. Perhaps you and Jett might like to see them before you head home? If you have time, that is.'

Sarah's surprise quickly turned to genuine

pleasure. 'We'd love that, Mr. Johnson.'

'Hugo, please,' he corrected. 'And afterwards, maybe Jett would like to help me pick out a spot for a special mango tree. One that would be just his to watch over.'

Jett's eyes widened with delight. 'Really? My very own tree?'

'Every member of this family has one,' Hugo explained seriously. 'It's tradition.'

Oliver felt a rush of gratitude toward his father—not for merely accepting Sarah and Jett, but for recognising what they might mean to his future.

Later, as Hugo showed Jett the different herbs with a patience Oliver rarely witnessed in his practical father, Sarah moved to stand beside Oliver.

'Your dad wasn't so sure about us at first,' she observed quietly.

'How could you tell?'

'I raised a child on my own,' Sarah replied with a small smile. 'You develop a sixth sense about these things.'

'He's coming around,' Oliver assured her.

Sarah nodded, watching Hugo lift Jett onto

his shoulders to better see the huge mango tree across the garden fence. 'That's Oli's tree,' he said.

'Oli?' Jett giggled. 'That's not his name.'

Family wasn't just given, Oliver realised. Sometimes it was carefully, thoughtfully built— one mango tree at a time.

'We should probably head home,' Sarah said eventually, noticing Jett's valiant but failing battle against sleep. 'It's well past his bedtime.'

'Of course,' Ellen agreed, though she looked reluctant to see them leave. 'But you must come back soon. Perhaps for Sunday lunch next week? We'll be more rested by then, less jet-lagged.'

'That's very kind,' Sarah began diplomatically.

'Let's not overwhelm them, Mum,' Oliver interjected, recognising Sarah's polite hesitation. 'They might need some recovery time from the Johnson experience.'

Ellen looked ready to protest, but Hugo placed a gentle hand on her arm. 'Oli's right, love. Let them breathe.'

The goodbyes were warm and slightly chaotic, with Ellen insisting on packing leftovers for them to take home and Grandmère extracting a promise from Sarah to share her lavender soap recipe "for comparison" with her cousin Mathilde's methods.

'I'll walk you to your car,' Oliver said, taking the container of leftovers from his mother before she could add yet another item to the already substantial care package.

The night air had cooled, and stars were brilliantly visible in the clear country sky. Jett, despite his tiredness, looked up in wonder.

'So many stars,' he whispered.

'More than you can count,' Oliver agreed, opening the car door so Sarah could settle Jett into his booster seat.

Once Jett was buckled in, already half-asleep, Oliver and Sarah stood beside the car, momentarily alone.

'I'm sorry if that was overwhelming,' Oliver said quietly.

'Don't apologise,' Sarah replied, her face softened by the dim glow of the porch light. 'They're wonderful. Exactly as you described them—loud, opinionated, but wonderful.'

'They liked you,' Oliver said. 'Both of you.'

'The feeling's mutual.' Sarah glanced back at the house. 'It's nice to see where you come from, who shaped you.'

Oliver nodded, feeling oddly vulnerable. There was something intimate about introducing Sarah to his family, to the farm that had been his whole world for so long.

'I was thinking,' he began, suddenly nervous. 'Would you like to go out sometime? Just the two of us?'

Sarah raised an eyebrow. 'Are you asking me on a proper date, Oliver Johnson?'

'I believe I am,' he confirmed, a smile tugging at his lips. 'Though it seems backwards, doesn't it? Meeting the family before our first non-blind date.'

'We've never done things in the conventional order,' Sarah reminded him. 'Why start now?'

Oliver laughed softly. 'True enough.'

'I'd love to,' she said. 'Elaine has been offering to babysit for weeks. She's frighteningly invested in our relationship.'

'She and Amelia should never meet,' Oliver said with mock horror. 'The combined force of their meddling would be unstoppable.'

Sarah's laugh was cut short as Oliver leaned down to kiss her, his hand gently cupping her cheek. Unlike their previous kisses, this one held the promise of something deeper, something taking root.

'Goodnight, Sarah,' he whispered when they finally parted.

'Goodnight, mango man,' she replied with a teasing smile.

Oliver stood in the driveway long after her taillights had disappeared down the dark country road, the farmhouse behind him alive with the sounds of his family, the orchard around him silent and steadfast. For the first time in years, the farm felt not just like his responsibility, but like a home he might someday share.

Epilogue

The early morning light filtered through the kitchen windows as Oliver checked his market crates one final time. The mangoes gleamed like jewels against their tissue paper nests—perfect, unblemished, each one selected with meticulous care. Market days had taken on new significance these past months, transformed from routine commerce to something he now looked forward to.

Amelia padded into the kitchen in her pyjamas, hair tousled and currently a subdued lavender—tame by her standards. She made directly for the coffee pot, pouring herself a generous mug before hopping onto the counter, legs dangling.

'You're up early,' Oliver observed, securing the last crate. 'Thought you'd be sleeping in after your late night.'

Amelia shrugged, blowing steam from her mug. 'Couldn't sleep.'

Something in her tone made Oliver pause. He studied his sister's face, noting the slight puffiness around her eyes. 'Everything all right?'

'Myron and I broke up,' she announced without preamble, taking a long sip of coffee.

'I'm sorry,' Oliver said, genuinely surprised. Unlike Amelia's usual brief entanglements, her relationship with the artistic barista had lasted more than three months—a record by her standards. 'What happened?'

'Nothing dramatic. We just want different things.' She attempted a casual tone that didn't quite succeed. 'He's moving to Brisbane next month. Wants to work in some fancy café where they charge fifteen dollars for avocado toast.'

Oliver leaned against the counter beside her. 'And you didn't want to go?'

'The farm's home,' Amelia said simply. 'I know I joke about leaving, about all the places I'll see, but . . .' She gestured vaguely toward the window where the early sun was painting the cane fields gold. 'It gets under your skin, doesn't it?'

Oliver nodded, understanding perfectly. 'It does.'

They sat in companionable silence for a moment, the only sounds the distant crow of a rooster and the gentle ticking of the kitchen clock.

'Maybe I need to put you on a dating app,' Oliver finally joked, nudging her shoulder gently. 'Return the favour.'

Amelia snorted into her coffee. 'Oh, what a brilliant idea. 'Farmer's sister seeks local man with flexible definition of normal hair colour, must tolerate excessive enthusiasm and strong opinions.''

'Could work,' Oliver grinned. 'You never know where you might find someone perfect for you.'

'Says the man who literally found his perfect match through an app that his sister hijacked,' Amelia retorted, but she was smiling now.

'Technically, I found her at the markets first,' Oliver corrected. 'The app was just a roundabout way back.'

'Semantics,' Amelia waved dismissively. 'The point is, you're disgustingly happy now.' She hopped down from the counter and rinsed her mug. 'Speaking of which, how's the farm weekend market idea coming along? Sarah seemed interested when I mentioned it last week.'

'We're discussing it,' Oliver said carefully. 'It's a big undertaking.'

'But brilliant,' Amelia insisted. 'Having craft vendors right here at the farm every other weekend would bring in a whole new customer base. Sarah's soaps, those honey people from Bargara, maybe even that woodworker with the cutting boards.' Her enthusiasm was returning, eyes brightening with each idea. 'We could start small, just a few stalls. See how it goes.'

Oliver smiled, recognising the familiar signs of an Amelia project gathering momentum. Perhaps it was exactly what she needed right now. 'I'll talk to Dad about it. And Guy.'

'Already did,' she admitted. 'They're on board. Dad thinks it's "innovative marketing" and Guy says the numbers look promising.'

'Of course you did,' Oliver laughed, shaking his head as he picked up the first crate. 'Let me get through today's market first, all right? One thing at a time.'

As he loaded the truck, Oliver found himself considering Amelia's idea more seriously. Having Sarah's craft stall here at the farm regularly would mean more time together, bridging their separate worlds in a way that felt right somehow. Worth considering, at least.

***

Three months later

'Higher, Uncle Oli! I can't reach it!' Jett called from beneath the mango tree, his small arms stretched toward a particularly fine specimen just beyond his grasp.

Oliver smiled at the boy's casual use of "uncle"—a title that had been given by Jett a few weeks ago and stuck, feeling more natural with each use. He reached up, easily plucking the mango and placing it in Jett's waiting hands.

'Careful with that one,' he instructed. 'It's perfect for the special display.'

Jett examined the fruit with expert concentration before gently placing it in his basket alongside others he'd collected. Five years old now, he'd become an authoritative judge of mango quality, much to the amusement of the weekend market customers who now regularly visited the farm.

Amelia's farm market idea had exceeded even her optimistic projections. What had started as a small gathering of five local vendors had quickly grown to fifteen regular stallholders, attracting visitors from as far as Bundaberg and Maryborough. The Johnson farm had transformed from a quiet agricultural operation to a bustling community hub every other weekend, with Sarah's craft stall as one of the central attractions.

'Mummy!' Jett called, spotting Sarah approaching through the orchard rows. 'Look how many I found!'

Sarah smiled, her hair pulled back in a loose braid, cheeks flushed from the summer heat. 'That's quite a haul. Are you leaving any for the customers?'

'Only the ordinary ones,' Jett assured her solemnly. 'I'm getting the special ones.'

'Of course you are,' Sarah laughed, meeting Oliver's gaze with shared amusement. 'Amelia's looking for you. Something about the parking arrangements for tomorrow's market.'

'I'll find her in a minute,' Oliver replied, watching as Jett darted ahead, carefully balancing his precious basket of mangoes. When the boy was safely out of earshot, Oliver reached for Sarah's hand, gently tugging her closer.

'How's the soap tent coming along?'

'All set,' she confirmed. 'The holiday collection is ready to launch. Elaine's helping with the display tomorrow.'

'You've been busy.'

'Says the man who's been up since dawn tending to his precious mangoes,' she teased.

Oliver smiled, taking in the sight of her—the woman who had transformed his life in ways he was still discovering. The past three months had unfolded with a natural rhythm that felt both surprising and inevitable. Sarah and Jett had become fixtures at the farm, first as weekend visitors, then staying for dinners, and gradually occupying more space in his heart than he'd known was available.

'Thank you,' he said suddenly, surprising himself with the intensity of feeling behind the simple words.

'For what?' Sarah asked, her expression softening.

'For showing me that love was worth the awkward journey,' Oliver replied, thinking of dating app disasters, misplaced phone numbers, and the winding path that had eventually led them back to each other. 'For taking a chance on a farmer who couldn't even handle a hot pepper without causing a scene.'

Sarah laughed, the sound still as captivating as the first time he'd heard it across a crowded market. 'That pepper story gets more dramatic with each telling.'

'It was traumatic,' Oliver insisted with mock seriousness. 'I nearly died of embarrassment.'

'Well, I'm glad you survived,' Sarah replied, standing on tiptoes to kiss him briefly. 'Jett and I have grown rather attached to you.'

The casual acknowledgment of their connection sent warmth spreading through Oliver's chest. He'd never been one for grand gestures or poetic declarations, preferring to let actions speak instead. But some moments, he was learning, called for a bit of both.

'Wait here,' he said, releasing her hand and moving toward a specific tree nearby. With practiced movements, he selected a perfect mango, its skin blushing golden-red in the afternoon sun.

In the distance, they could hear Jett chattering excitedly to Amelia about his mango selections, the farm bustling with pre-market preparations. But for this moment, standing amidst the orchard rows where their story had begun, there was only the two of them— connected by that peculiar magic of finding your way back to where you were always meant to be.

'Mum! Uncle Oli!' Jett's voice broke the spell as he came running back. 'Grandmère says to come quick! She's making crepes with the mangoes!'

Oliver laughed, catching Sarah's eye with a shared look of affectionate resignation. 'We'd better not keep Grandmère waiting. She gets, shall we say, creative when she's impatient.'

As they walked hand in hand toward the farmhouse, following Jett's excited lead, contentment settled over Oliver. The journey had been unexpected, occasionally awkward, and entirely worth every step.

Later that evening, after Jett had devoured two of Grandmère's crepes and charmed the entire Johnson family with his enthusiastic questions about the farm, Sarah found him sitting alone on the porch steps, small hands wrapped around a mango, his expression unusually serious.

'Hey, sweetie,' Sarah said, settling beside him on the step. 'Everything okay?'

Jett nodded, but continued studying the mango with intense concentration.

'It's been quite a day,' Sarah offered, gently brushing his hair from his forehead. 'Lots of new people to meet.'

'Mm-hmm.' Jett rolled the mango between his palms, a habit he'd picked up from Oliver. 'Uncle Oli's family is big.'

Sarah's heart warmed at his casual use of 'Uncle Oli,' a name he'd adopted without prompting a few weeks ago. 'They are big. And a little loud sometimes. Does that bother you?'

Jett shook his head. 'I like them. Grandmère tells funny stories, and Amelia said I could help her collect the eggs tomorrow.' He paused, his small face scrunching in thought. 'Mom, does Uncle Oli live here all the time?'

'Yes, this is his home. He lives here with his family, just like we live in our house.'

Jett seemed to contemplate this information carefully. 'And we live in our house.'

'That's right.'

'But you like Uncle Oli a lot.' It wasn't a question, but a statement of fact, delivered with the directness only children can manage.

Sarah felt her cheeks warm. 'Yes, I do like him. Very much.'

Jett nodded solemnly, as if confirming a suspicion. 'I saw you kissing him by the mango trees. Like people do on TV.'

Sarah bit back a smile. 'You did, huh?'

'Uh-huh.' Jett looked up at her finally, his eyes serious. 'Does that mean he's gonna be your boyfriend now?'

Sarah weighed her words carefully. 'Would that be okay with you if he was?'

Jett returned his attention to the mango, turning it over in his hands. 'I guess. He knows a lot about mangoes and chickens and stuff.' He paused, his voice growing quieter. 'But what about our house? What about my room with the dinosaur wallpaper?'

The question revealed the real concern hiding beneath his casual inquiries, and Sarah wrapped an arm around his shoulders. 'Oh, sweetheart. Nothing's going to happen to our house or your dinosaur room. Uncle Oli and I are just getting to know each other better.'

'But Damon at daycare said when his mum got a boyfriend, they moved to a new house, and he had to share a room with a new brother he didn't even like.' Jett's voice wavered slightly. 'And he couldn't take his special bookshelf because it didn't fit.'

Sarah pulled him closer. 'Every family is different, Jett. Whatever happens between me and Oliver, I promise we won't make any big changes without talking to you first. Your happiness matters very much to me.'

From the doorway, Oliver watched the quiet exchange, careful to remain unnoticed. He'd come looking for them when Sarah had been gone longer than expected, only to halt at the sound of his name.

'But do you love him?' Jett was asking, his voice small but determined. 'Like in the stories?'

Sarah's reply was gentle. 'It's still early days, sweetie. Love takes time to grow, just like the mangoes on Uncle Oli's trees.'

Jett considered this, then offered his next question with disarming innocence. 'Does he make you happy? Your eyes get all crinkly when he's around. Like when you eat chocolate cake.'

Sarah laughed softly. 'Yes, he does make me happy.'

'That's good then,' Jett decided, apparently satisfied with her answer. 'Because you should be happy, Mum. But I still don't want a new brother.'

'Noted,' Sarah said solemnly, though her lips twitched with amusement. 'No new brothers on the horizon.'

Oliver stepped back silently, giving them a moment longer before he deliberately made his footsteps audible as he approached. 'There you two are. Grandmère's asking if Jett wants to help her make hot chocolate. Apparently, it's a 'secret French recipe.''

Jett perked up immediately. 'With marshmallows?'

'Knowing Grandmère, probably with some fancy French chocolate she smuggled in her suitcase.'

Jett looked to his mother for permission, suddenly vibrating with renewed energy.

'Go ahead,' Sarah smiled. 'Just don't drink too much or you'll be bouncing off the walls all night.'

As Jett raced inside, Oliver settled onto the step beside Sarah. 'Everything okay? You two looked deep in conversation.'

Sarah leaned against his shoulder with a sigh. 'Just navigating the complex emotional terrain of being a single parent who's dating.'

'Ah,' Oliver nodded. 'The boyfriend talk?'

'Complete with concerns about moving houses and acquiring unwanted siblings.' She glanced up at him. 'For the record, I assured him his dinosaur room was safe.'

Oliver chuckled, but there was a tenderness in his eyes as he looked at her. 'Kids notice everything, don't they?'

'Especially the things we think we're being subtle about.' She touched his hand lightly. 'He said I should be with you because you make my eyes crinkly like when I eat chocolate cake.'

'High praise indeed,' Oliver said, taking her hand in his. 'I'll do my best to keep those eyes crinkling.'

'He'll need time,' Sarah said quietly. 'To adjust to sharing me. To understand that this doesn't change how much I love him.'

'We have all the time in the world,' Oliver assured her. 'No rush, no pressure. We'll figure it out together, the three of us.'

Jett's excited voice drifted out to them as he recounted something to Grandmère, followed by her delightful laughter.

'You're good with him,' Sarah said softly. 'Most men I've dated couldn't see past the "single mother" label to the actual child behind it. He was just an obstacle, or worse, an afterthought.'

'Those men were idiots,' Oliver stated simply. 'Jett's not just part of the package, Sarah. He's amazing in his own right. Smart, curious, enthusiastic about mangoes—what's not to love?'

Sarah smiled, leaning into him as the evening air cooled around them. 'You Johnson men have a way with words when it counts.'

'Only when it matters,' Oliver replied, dropping a kiss on the top of her head. 'Only when it matters.'

Coming in June: Book 4: Chasing Dreams

When Elena Santiago joins the Johnsons' seasonal crew at the cane farm in Duckinwilla Creek, she plans to stay only three months—just long enough to complete the final leg of her journey before returning to Brazil to reshape her family's fifth-generation farm. But when Guy Johnson meets the quiet, confident woman with bright ideas and a love of the land, something shifts. As they work together on the farm, their professional respect slowly deepens as they work together.

As Elena's departure draws near, Guy faces a choice he never expected: hold on to the comfort of the familiar or follow the woman who's quietly captured his heart.

Pre-order in **eBook:**
https://books2read.com/u/bwxkMP
Print:
https://annieseatonstore.ecwid.com/Chasing-Dreams-Book-4-Duckinwilla-Days-PRE-ORDER-p743060505

Also by Annie Seaton

Daughters of the Darling
From Across the Sea
Over the River
By the Billabong
Beneath Still Waters

A Bec Whitfield Mystery
Bowen River
Shadows on the Shore

Duckinwilla Days
Coming Home
Secrets and Surprises
Wishes and Whispers

Home to the Outback
Lucy
Angie
Jemima
Isabella

Porter Sisters Series
Kakadu Sunset
Daintree

Diamond Sky
Hidden Valley
Larapinta
Kakadu Dawn

Others
Whitsunday Dawn
Undara
Osprey Reef
East of Alice
One Summer in Tuscany
Four Seasons Short and Sweet
Follow the Sun
Ten Days in Paradise
Deadly Secrets
Adventures in Time
Silver Valley Witch
The Emerald Necklace
A Clever Christmas
Christmas with the Boss
Her Christmas Star
The Emerald Necklace

The Augathella Girls Series
Outback Roads
Outback Sky
Outback Escape

Outback Wind
Outback Dawn
Outback Moonlight
Outback Dust
Outback Hope
Boxed Sets
Augathella Girls 1-4
Augathella Girls 5-8

Augathella Short and Sweet Series
An Augathella Surprise
An Augathella Baby
An Augathella Spring
An Augathella Christmas
An Augathella Wedding
An Augathella Easter
An Augathella Masquerade Ball
Boxed Set
Augathella Short and Sweet 1-3

Sunshine Coast Series
Waiting for Ana
The Trouble with Jack
Healing His Heart
Sunshine Coast Boxed Set

The Richards Brothers Series

The Trouble with Paradise
Marry in Haste
Outback Sunrise
Richards Brothers Boxed Set
Bondi Beach Love Series
Beach House
Beach Music
Beach Walk
Beach Dreams
The House on the Hill Boxed Set

Second Chance Bay Series
Her Outback Playboy
Her Outback Protector
Her Outback Haven
Her Outback Paradise
Boxed Set
The McDougalls of Second Chance Bay Boxed Set

Love Across Time Series
Come Back to Me
Follow Me
Finding Home
The Threads that Bind
Boxed Set
Love Across Time 1-4

Bindarra Creek
Worth the Wait
Full Circle
Secrets of River Cottage
A Clever Christmas
A Place to Belong
Hearts in Harmony

Annie lives in Australia, on the beautiful north coast of New South Wales. She sits in her writing chair and looks out over the tranquil Pacific Ocean.

She writes contemporary romance and loves telling stories that always have a happily ever after. She lives with her very own hero of many years, and they share their home with Barney, the rag doll puss, who hides when the four grandchildren come to visit.

Stay up to date with her latest releases at her website: **http://www.annieseaton.net**

If you would like to stay up to date with Annie's releases, subscribe to her newsletter here: http://www.annieseaton.net